I've travelled the world twice over,
Met the famous: saints and sinners,
Poets and artists, kings and queens,
Old stars and hopeful beginners,
I've been where no-one's been before,
Learned secrets from writers and cooks
All with one library ticket
To the wonderful world of books.

© JANICE JAMES.

KING'S FOLLY

When Jessica Milroy — divorced, ageing, but still energetic — attempts to have a much-deserved holiday, her foray into the West Country in her small, unreliable car results in an extraordinary experience. Meeting many characters very different from those she had encountered during her somewhat conventional life, she is caught up in their problems to such a degree that to solve them becomes an obsession. When, inadvertently, she is presented with the answer she has long been seeking, it is as unexpected as it is tragic.

PAMELA STREET

KING'S FOLLY

Complete and Unabridged

ULVERSCROFT
Leicester

First published in Great Britain in 1995 by
Robert Hale Limited
London

First Large Print Edition
published 1996
by arrangement with
Robert Hale Limited
London

British Library CIP Data

Street, Pamela, *1921* –
  King's Folly.—Large print ed.—
  Ulverscroft large print series: general fiction
  1. English fiction—20th century
  2. Large type books
  I. Title
  823.9′14 [F]

  ISBN 0–7089–3657–1

Published by
F. A. Thorpe (Publishing) Ltd.
Anstey, Leicestershire
Set by Words & Graphics Ltd.
Anstey, Leicestershire
Printed and bound in Great Britain by
T. J. Press (Padstow) Ltd., Padstow, Cornwall

This book is printed on acid-free paper

1

AFTER her sixtieth birthday, Jessica Milroy began paying much more attention to the Death columns in her daily paper, rather than the ones which announced Births and Marriages. By the time she was sixty-five, interest in the first had completely overtaken the other two.

Funny, she thought, one morning in the early nineteen nineties, as she ran her eyes down the list of those who had received their marching orders — as her irreverent grandson was apt to put it — that one did not think about death very much at Jason's age unless, of course, one had been unlucky enough to have had some personal experience of it. Life appeared to stretch out before the young, lots and lots of it, *ad infinitum*. They got into cars, never doubting that they would reach their destinations safely and soundly. But nowadays, Jessica never felt quite sure of getting anywhere. The awful fragility of existence seemed to challenge her daily. Steering her own little car round Hyde Park Corner or along a motorway was enough to send her blood pressure up. She knew it was silly to think like this, because what did it matter if, at her age, she failed to get wherever she was going, so long as she did not harm anyone else in the process. She was old, expendable, past her sell-by date.

Besides, Jessica mused, my family is so ridiculously small. No one is depending on me. It's not as if I have to be in *loco parentis* for Jason any more. *One* day my name will simply be added to the list I've just been studying.

She could almost visualise it. She could also recall having been rather ashamed of once actually making a few jottings in an old notebook: *MILROY — On* ?, *Jessica Frances,* aged ? (perhaps not, unless I reach 90 which is highly unlikely), *loving mother of Simon* ? (hardly, more like exasperated, difficult this one), *devoted grandmother of Jason* (certainly). *Funeral private. No flowers* (why no flowers? I love flowers). *Family flowers only* (but

2

I hardly *have* any family. No sisters or brothers, one son, one grandson, one daughter-in-law, no two, if you count Simon's second wife). What about *Donations if desired* . . . ? No, better not. It's like blackmail, putting all the onus on the consciences of friends and acquaintances.

Jessica remembered how she had occasionally had to struggle with her own conscience under such circumstances. How much shall I send? Shall I send anything? Who will know if I don't except, perhaps, the undertaker and the departed? But I don't believe in an after-life, do I? It isn't as if old Admiral Williams is going to look down from heaven watching me write the cheque. Anyway, why am I bothering with all this? It's indulgent, satisfying my passion for orderliness, desire to control. It will be up to Simon to see to everything. I shan't be there. I'll have slipped behind those ghastly curtain things in the crematorium, probably in a ridiculously expensive coffin. Simon will be all for the look of the thing. He'll probably come flying back from wherever he is and want to do it *his* way. *I* may want a private funeral, but he'll want a champagne send-off, rather like launching a ship down a slipway. Will he mind that Jason gets the bulk of my estate, that I've left all my jewellery to Marianne, his mother, who I am fond of, instead of to Helen, his stepmother, who I am not?

With an effort, Jessica laid aside the daily paper and told herself to stop being morbid and think positively, especially now, for she was at a crossroads. Two days ago, the man for whom she had worked for fifteen years, Gerald Frobisher, had suddenly informed her that he would no longer require her services. He explained that he had lost a lot of money through Lloyds and was going to sell up and go abroad. Just like that. No preamble. No saying he was sorry. But then he wasn't that sort of person. She had never understood him. He was a widower, remote, often away and, when in residence, wrapped up in the antiquarian books through which, until now, she had imagined he made his living; although she had occasionally suspected that his late wife, about whom he rarely spoke, might have been wealthy.

There had never been anything of a romantic nature between Gerald Frobisher and herself. Far from it. It was one of those surprising and unlikely relationships which happened to work. He had asked her in the beginning what he should call her, and she had simply replied, 'Jessica'. He had never suggested that she should call him Gerald. When she had told friends of this formal behaviour, she knew they scarcely believed her. Jason had thought it a huge joke, but Marianne had said more than once that she thought Jessica's employer treated her in rather a cavalier fashion. "It's best to go on as we started," was all Jessica could say. "I could no more think of calling Gerald Frobisher by his Christian name than I could think of calling my bank manager Fred. We have a purely business arrangement and we both prefer to keep it that way. It was an amazing stroke of luck to have got the job in the first place."

Indeed, Jessica had never been able to forget that. At the age of fifty, having finally summoned up courage to leave Simon's father for the same reason as Marianne had divorced Simon — only at a much earlier stage of their marriage — Jessica had fled to London to the small *pied-à-terre*, where she suspected William had conducted many an affair. She had not meant to stay there for any length of time. She had intended to return to Scotland, somewhere near, but not too near, the home where she had lived for twenty-five years. But circumstances or, rather, Mr Holt, her late parents' solicitor, obliged her to remain in London while the divorce went through. "You have, in fact, done something rather clever, Jessica," he said. "Clever?" she had queried, feeling far from clever and very far from the safety of her familiar surroundings. "Yes," came Archie Holt's prompt reply. "You see, technically, you have not left the marital home, the flat being a part of it. This is a point in your favour. I strongly advise you to stay where you are while we negotiate a satisfactory settlement." "Settlement?" she remembered asking. "But I want a divorce, as soon as possible."

Now that she had surprised herself by having taken such an enormous step, Mr Holt's cautious approach to the matter seemed frustrating although, grudgingly, she realised his next words made sense. "Of course you want to get on with things. But we must consider what financial support you will need. That's what divorce is all about, isn't it? You are not independent. While you are in the flat we must see that your husband pays all the outgoings and you must be adequately provided for after that. Preferably, I feel that the lease of the second marital establishment should be made over to you. We must be certain that you will have absolute security before any decrees are passed."

She had gone away from Messrs Holt and Bellinger saddened and bewildered. She was not an avaricious woman, nor an extravagant one. She had vaguely imagined that William would provide her with the wherewithal to buy some small house on the outskirts of Edinburgh, where she would live cheaply and simply. She did not like London. She had rarely made use of the Kensington flat which he had insisted on buying. She had always maintained that she was too busy bringing up Simon and, once their son had gone to boarding-school, the pattern seemed to have been set. She had used the flat just at the moment because William was abroad and it was a convenient bolt-hole from which she could consult Archie Holt. She had no wish to remain any longer than necessary in the place — and certainly not the bedroom — where she suspected her husband must have committed adultery with a whole string of nubile ladies. Her whole being cried out for the known, the familiar.

On her way back to Kensington that afternoon, she had wandered into the local library, staving off the time when she knew she would sit looking out over the London rooftops at the hundreds of lighted windows behind which, she imagined, everyone else would be in twos or threes or maybe having a party. She was sure no one would be staring out *alone*.

The librarian on duty, a pleasant-looking girl who reminded her of a younger Marianne, told Jessica that in order to take out books she would have to register as a resident in the district, producing some kind of evidence to this effect. Jessica nodded. She felt too weary to ask the procedure for temporary residents. It seemed too much trouble. She simply wandered out again but, at the door, her eyes caught sight of an advertisement pinned on a notice board. Afterwards, she realised how easily she might have missed seeing it. The fact that she did not seemed like some kind of omen. WANTED, she read:

Secretary. Elastic hours. Reliability essential. Suit older woman. FROBISHER, Flat 3, Oswestry Mansions. SW7. Tel. 587 5849.

Oswestry Mansions, Jessica said to herself. Why, that's just round the corner from where I'm living. How extraordinary. If I really have to sit tight for a bit, as Archie Holt says, it would certainly give me something to do. My typing's a bit rusty and I've almost forgotten the shorthand I learned as a girl. But it seems this Frobisher chap is

9

keener on other qualifications. Of course, I'd have to explain about only being temporary. That'll probably put me out of the running. But the *proximity*. Only half a minute's walk. Maybe I could just fill in while Mr Frobisher looks around for someone permanent.

And that was how it had started.

Despite all the odds stacked against the initial tentative arrangement — Jessica's desire to return to Scotland, the distress of Archie Holt who found himself acting for a client who was actually earning money while he was trying to plead poverty, a certain amount of gossip, even at one stage an insulting enquiry from a top barrister as to whether she was being kept — her job with Gerald Frobisher became permanent. It was a set-up which suited them both, especially after Marianne had left Simon and was alone with a lively young son to bring up. Jessica discovered she could be of enormous support to her daughter-in-law by caring for the child as much as possible while his mother, courageously, found herself some rented accommodation in Clapham and went back to part-time teaching. Between them, thanks to the 'elastic hours' which Jessica was able to work, often doing much of it in her own home, they brought Jason up.

In many ways, Jessica felt as if she had been given a second chance in life: a second chance at looking after a small boy again, possibly making a better job of being a grandmother than she had ever done as a mother. She felt happy, independent. She was *Jessica* Milroy, instead of the wife of William Milroy, womaniser and not particularly assiduous head of a firm of glass manufacturers, which gave him the excuse for constantly visiting London and other capitals, ostensibly to promote his wares. "It's so important, Jess," he would say, "to keep Milroys' name in the forefront, to let the buyers know what we have to offer, maintain contact, all that sort of thing." At the beginning of their marriage, in her naïveté and because she was in love, she had believed him. It was only some years after Simon had been born that she came to realise that the 'contacts' were of a very different kind from those he had specified.

After she had left him and been granted the lease of the flat thanks, Jessica had to admit, to the most patient and tenacious efforts on the part of her solicitor, she found, much to her surprise, that she really liked living in London. Her job, her involvement with Jason, the relief of no longer bothering about William and where he was or what he was doing, seemed to take years off her life. She was fortunate in never having gone grey and, now, some of her youthful good looks and *joie de vivre* seemed to have returned. Once or twice she had gone back to see friends in Scotland who had remarked on this, but her visits became less frequent and only served to make her realise how complete was the severance between her former life and her new one.

Apart from a few short bucket and spade holidays with Marianne and Jason, she had taken no other breaks. Gerald Frobisher never remarked on this and although she felt he might have shown a little more appreciation of her constancy, she did not let it bother her. She knew she was invaluable to him, that his advertisement for a 'reliable older woman' all that time ago, had paid off handsomely. Like his cleaning lady of longstanding, she had the keys of his home. He himself could go away at a moment's notice on one of his book-finding jaunts knowing that everything could be left safely in her hands. She would enter his large somewhat stuffy and over-furnished flat daily, sometimes bringing Jason with her — something to which, considering his aloof professorial manner and the many valuable books he had lying around, she was pleased to find he never raised any objection. She opened his post, checked his answering machine for any messages, watered his plants and got in touch with him if she thought it necessary. He always paid her exactly the same, however short or long a week she worked. Over the years, this set amount had risen. It was not, perhaps exactly generous, but it seemed perfectly adequate.

She had never had any inclination to go away on holiday alone. She supposed it was unenterprising of her, but she could not bear the thought of sitting down at a table by herself in some hotel dining-room or soaking up the sun in some foreign clime. Unlike her peripatetic ex-husband, son and second daughter-in-law, she did not like 'abroad'; while the thought of doing nothing appalled her. She remembered reading somewhere that Mrs Thatcher, as she then was, had been travelling through some holiday resort and had noticed a whole lot of people lying on a beach. "Whatever are they doing?" she asked one of her aides. And well she might, Jessica had thought. What on earth *were* they doing? Or thinking, for that matter? They would hardly have been asleep. Comatose, perhaps, vaguely aware of bodily sensations, but little else. Jessica supposed that it was what the medical fraternity meant when it talked about relaxing and imagined that possibly the fact she had never gone in for it was the reason she suffered from slightly high blood pressure.

Now, with Gerald Frobisher having just dropped his bombshell, she wondered whether, after all, it wasn't high time to rethink her ideas. She would scarcely find another job at her age, let alone one which suited her so well. But she would have to fill her days somehow. Jason had left school. Marianne had remarried and was living in Surrey. William had died but, thanks to the foresight of Archie Holt, a Deed of Covenant had been drawn up at the time of the divorce, entitling her to a fairly substantial sum on her husband's death. This was to be the first charge on his estate and though, due to William's lifestyle, he had left far less than might have been expected, Jessica's share was honoured. There was really no need for her to go on working. On the face of it, there was every reason for her to retire gracefully, alter course. The time had come, in fact, to take another leap in faith, just as she had done fifteen years ago.

But I was younger then, she said to herself. Any change would be much more difficult now. I may have kept my wits about me, but I know I've slowed up. I shall have to think, and think hard. Perhaps I *should* go away, if it's only to do the thinking.

Although just where an elderly, lone, xenophobic, redundant female should go under these circumstances, I'm blessed if I know.

2

"KING'S FOLLY can be highly recommended," said the young man with an earring in one ear, sitting behind the desk at the local Tourist Board. "In fact, the owners have recently expanded their establishment. They used to do just B and B, but they've now turned their dairy into first-class family accommodation. I think they call it the Daye House, something to do with being the old-fashioned word for dairy. It has a small kitchenette. They still do breakfasts, but they now provide picnics plus an evening meal. Mrs King's a cordon bleu cook. It's pricey, of course, especially if it's taken over by one person, but well worth it."

"Does the name of the farm have something to do with the owners?" Jessica enquired.

The young man seemed to think this highly amusing. "Why, no. I believe it's been called that for yonks. Probably some

17

king holed up there. Alfred, I shouldn't wonder. Or maybe one of the Charles'." He giggled slightly and she felt she had asked a stupid question.

"How far away is it?" She tried to get the conversation on a more business-like footing.

"Let me see. About fifteen miles, I think."

"Have you actually been there yourself?"

"Me?" He raised his eyebrows, obviously surprised, even shocked at the question. "Oh, no. But our inspector has, naturally. Beautiful countryside. I think you mentioned something about painting?"

"Yes." She began to feel more and more doubtful about what she was doing. Bringing her old painting things had simply been an afterthought. She wasn't quite sure what had motivated her into touring the West Country, only that after her last somewhat traumatic day working for Gerald Frobisher — who had actually seemed much more human than usual, surprising her by saying he was sorry that owing to his financial difficulties he was unable to give her a golden handshake — she had been determined to leave

London as soon as possible, but in a way which did not tie her down. No booking up. No buying of tickets. No flying off to foreign parts. Not even a cruise up the Nile, as Marianne had suggested.

She had found Simon's first wife's concern for her welfare rather touching. "If you're touring, Ma," Marianne had said, "we shan't be able to keep tabs on you." Jessica had not been aware that anyone would want to keep tabs on her. "I'll certainly keep in touch," she had promised, "ring and let you know how things are going. Setting off for a part of England I've hardly seen will be . . . well, quite an adventure. I shall avoid the motorways. Just stop where my fancy takes me. If I find I don't like it, I'll simply move on or come straight back to London. I'll be quite free, as it were." As she said the word, Jessica realised how much freedom now meant to her.

Becoming suddenly aware that the earringed young man was waiting for her to make a decision, she said, quickly, "Perhaps you would telephone Mr and Mrs King and see if the dairy . . . er, the Daye House, is free."

"Certainly, madam," he replied, all at once deferential, pleased to think that, with any luck, he would soon have placed another client satisfactorily. He may not have seen King's Folly himself, but he felt Mrs Milroy was the kind of older sensible woman who would be sure to appreciate upmarket accommodation.

Jessica waited while he picked up the receiver beside him and heard, quite clearly, a foreign voice, loud and excitable, on the other end of the line. "Meeses King. She pick fruit. Meester King gone doctor. Yes, Daye house all empty. Free tonight. What is lady called, pliz?" There was now some difficulty in getting the name of Milroy across to whoever was answering the telephone at King's Folly, but Jessica was relieved and somewhat amused at the final words, "I tell Meeses King, Meelroy, lady. In hour's time."

The young man replaced the receiver and beamed. "All arranged," he said. "I expect you'd like directions."

"Thank you, yes. I have a fairly large-scale map, but perhaps you have a local one which might be better."

"Certainly." He selected one from a pile on his desk, opened it and frowned. Then he said, "If you'll just excuse me. I think perhaps my ... er, colleague's father-in-law who was born in these parts ... " He disappeared for a moment and returned with an older man who, in a deep West Country burr, remarked, in an almost accusatory manner, "You want to go up Folly, then?"

"Yes. I'd be grateful if you'd be kind enough to show me the best way to get there. I understand it's about fifteen miles away."

"All of that," he replied. "The road peters out towards the end. You have to open a gate on to a grass track. Some people are put off by that, 'specially if they've got a new car."

"That's no problem. Mine's an old rattle-trap."

"Well, it's up to you, but the place is right up back of beyond, if you see my meaning."

She wondered what on earth he was doing in a Tourist Board. Whereas the younger man had at least done his best to sell her King's Folly, this older one

21

seemed somehow anxious to put her off going there. She felt he could hardly be the inspector who had recommended the place, but she decided to ask him if he knew it.

He gave a short ejaculation, somewhere between a snort and a laugh. "Know it? 'Course I know it. I worked there sometime back. I was head dairyman, 'afore the Kings went in for diversifying."

"Diversifying?" She knew the word. She read the papers and was vaguely aware that farmers were doing much more than farming these days because they were hard up. But the reason, the technicalities of the situation, escaped her. She was a townswoman, woefully ignorant, she supposed, of what went on in the countryside.

"Yus," her gruff informant went on. "The Kings have lost a packet." Somehow he seemed to relish imparting this revelation. "'Course, they came into farming at the wrong time. Didn't know the fust thing about it. Things went from bad to wuss. They kept choppin' and changin'. First it was corn and cows. Then the Government said as how there was too much production goin' on. You must 'ave heard of them butter mountains and grain mountains, although why no one can get the food to them that's starving, beats me. Then, of course, there was that mad cow disease which fairly put the wind up a lot of farmers. But by that time the Kings had switched to chickens, until Mrs Currie and her salmonella poisoning put paid to that. So they sold off a fairish bit of land and went in for this catering caper. At least, Mrs King has."

"I see," Jessica said, although she did not really see. All she could think of was that she was glad she had only arranged to stay one night at King's Folly. The owners did not seem a very satisfactory couple. Their home seemed more than appropriately named, even if it did originate from some unfortunate king. I can leave tomorrow, Jessica said to herself, as she watched their ex-dairyman's none too clean finger pointing out the route she should take. Then he folded up the map and presented it to her with a final, but far from encouraging remark, "Good job it's summer time. You'd never find it in the dark."

She got up and made her way out to the car, wondering what role he played at the Tourist Board. Seeing that he had been an agricultural worker, it seemed odd that he was now, to all intents and purposes, evidently employed in a clerical capacity. Or perhaps, he, too, had diversified, only more successfully than the owners of King's Folly. He obviously had a grudge against them and was probably much better at boosting the amenities of other establishments.

Slowly and carefully, she drove off along his recommended route, stopping only once to consult the map, for his instructions had been detailed and graphic. "You want to slow down at Barnard's Corner," he had said, "where you'll see a sheet of water. That's the gravel pits, although there's precious little gravel left now. The place is being developed into some kind of nature reserve with an artificial lake and what have you. Then you come to Folly Bottom. You wants to rev up a bit there. It's a pretty steep climb up to the farmhouse. In winter that lower road is a quagmire. The Kings bought their place at this time of year. That's where they made their fust big mistake. No one wanting to take on a country property should do that. Stands to reason. Come winter and it's always a very different story."

She could see what he meant, especially after driving up through a veritable gorge to where a notice proclaimed: 'KING'S FOLLY. Please shut gate'. Having passed through it and did as she was bidden, she set off again along a rough track. She was just enough of a country woman to recognise that the cattle grazing on either side were steers. The scenery was beautiful now. She had emerged from the deep green shelter of woods to an expanse of upland, where the setting sun caught the mullioned windows of the farmhouse in the distance, so that they seemed to be winking at her as she drove the last half mile.

The thing which struck her most forcibly, however, as she stopped the car and walked towards the front door was the extreme quietness of the place.

In her urban mind, she somehow felt that there should at least have been a dog barking or some animal mooing or grunting, even, perhaps, a child or two. Yet it was strangely silent as she pulled on the bell and heard it jangle somewhere in the background. Then she waited, wondering whether it would be Mr or Mrs King who would greet her, or maybe the foreigner who had come on the line at the Tourist Board.

A spare, deeply-tanned man of about forty, immaculately dressed in fawn trousers, white shirt and white trainers, answered the door and, holding out his hand, said in an extremely pleasant voice, "Ah, you must be our new guest. Welcome to King's Folly." He did not look or sound anything like Jessica's idea of a farmer, more like the kind of person she imagined one might meet in a smart resort on the Riviera. Nevertheless, she said, "Good evening, Mr King," hoping that her surprise was not too evident.

"Oh, forgive me. I should have explained," he replied, apologetically. "I'm not Leonard. He's gone to bed. I'm just doing the honours."

26

"I'm so sorry. I do hope Mr King isn't ill." She remembered now how the excited foreigner on the telephone had mentioned something about a doctor.

"No. Not really. Leonard often goes to bed at this time." Jessica thought the voice sounded a little wary now. "Caroline, that's his wife, is cooking your dinner. She's asked me to take you over to the Daye House. I'm Chancy, by the way."

"Oh, I see. Thank you." She was annoyed at the way she seemed constantly to be saying, 'I see', when all the time she felt further and further from seeing anything at all. Was this man some kind of guest? He must be well known to his host and hostess, considering the use of their Christian names.

As if sensing her puzzlement, Chancy continued, as he picked up her overnight bag, "I live in that caravan you can see over there." He pointed in a westerly direction. "I came here some time ago, just for bed and breakfast, but then I stuck. I'm part of the establishment, you might say. Leo and Caro have been kind enough to tell me I'm useful. I suppose you'd call me an odd job man."

She laughed. With his bright blue eyes and amused expression, she realised that he might be invaluable to the Kings, especially if Leonard was in poor health. But, as she unpacked, took a bath and waited for the meal which Chancy predicted would arrive at eight p.m., or thereabouts, she couldn't help feeling that she had stumbled on a set-up which was more than a little unusual.

3

AN extraordinarily beautiful woman brought Jessica her dinner. She felt that there could be no question of mistaken identity this time. She could only be her hostess, Caroline, although she appeared so very much younger than Jessica had imagined.

She arrived at the door of the Daye House via a covered way, pushing a trolley which Jessica recognised as being one which kept food hot or cold, except that this looked far more attractive and superior than anything encountered in an ordinary communal establishment, such as a hospital. In fact, everything she had seen at King's Folly so far had suggested care, comfort and attention to detail, as if the whole place had been renovated by someone with an extremely aesthetic taste. It seemed a shame that apparently there was only she herself staying there at the moment to appreciate it all. Jessica could not help wondering whether the Kings' venture into accommodating paying guests was really paying off.

"I'm sorry," Caroline said, as she pushed the trolley through the front door and propelled it into the sitting-room, "I'm afraid I'm a little late. I spent too long picking strawberries. I'm so glad you're here. The couple we had over the weekend left yesterday. It's lovely to have the Daye booked up again."

Her charm, sincerity and artlessness were captivating. Jessica seldom remembered being so instantly drawn towards anyone in her life. She felt that the absent Leonard, presumably now holed up in bed, was a very lucky man.

"Please don't apologise. It's a great treat to have a meal cooked by someone else."

"You live alone then?" The naïveté Jessica had imagined suddenly seemed to evaporate. This woman might seem fey, but she was no fool. With her huge grey eyes, blonde hair pulled back into a pony tail, sleeveless T-shirt and long legs in skin-tight blue jeans, it seemed possible that she was the driving force behind whatever kept King's Folly ticking over.

"Yes," Jessica answered, "I used to quite enjoy cooking before . . . before I was divorced, but I don't find self-catering exactly . . . well, edifying. I'm afraid I'm now all too apt to buy frozen stuff. You know, boil-in-the-bag fish."

"Then I hope you'll find this a pleasant escape. I'm sorry you'll only be staying for one night. There are quite a lot of amenities round here which don't immediately hit the eye."

"Well, you've a wonderful view for a start, but tell me about all the others."

"I will. But right now I think you should eat your dinner. When I come to collect the remains, perhaps we might go into that."

Sensible, quick and tactful, Jessica thought, as she lifted the lids of various dishes, realising that the cuisine alone must surely be a five-star attraction: cold vichyssoise, lamb cutlets, new potatoes, peas and baby carrots, obviously from the garden, a strawberry meringue pie with clotted cream — presumably the strawberries being the ones referred to by both the foreign voice on the telephone and Caroline herself. There was also a half bottle of white wine in an ice bucket, together with a corkscrew and three little notes, one explaining the facilities in the minute kitchenette, another in the form of a questionnaire to be filled in regarding breakfast requirements, and a third — despite the installation of a mini-bar — saying *Wine on the House, First night bonus.* More than ever, Jessica felt that the owners of King's Folly were not exactly cut out for business.

When Caroline returned an hour or so later, she was accompanied by a large golden retriever. Jessica remarked that she had been surprised not to have seen a dog around the place before.

"Oh, Gracie wasn't here when you arrived. She was taking Mercedes home."

"Mercedes?" Jessica could only think of a make of car.

"Yes. Our Portuguese helper. In the summer she lives with her son and his wife and their little daughter down in Folly Bottom, but she goes back to Portugal in October. You probably didn't notice their cottage on the way up. This time of year it's pretty well hidden by trees. I don't think Mercedes approves of her daughter-in-law very much, so what with not liking Muriel nor the English winter it seems a sensible arrangement. She's also a bit nervous and excitable, so we're glad for Gracie to escort her home in the evenings. It's a bit lonely up here, as you can imagine. One day Gracie simply trotted after her as she left and it became a habit. Now she just takes her to the door of the cottage and Mercedes says, 'Go home now', and back comes Gracie under the stile by the gate you came through, and then barks to be let in."

Caroline gave the dog an affectionate pat, while continuing, "Although I'm not exactly sure how good a defence she'd be, if needed. Too sloppy. I think you'd say her presence is more of a comfort than anything else. Certainly to me . . . and to all of us," she added, as an afterthought.

Jessica found herself becoming more intrigued by the minute: a dog which acted as a kind of nanny, an excitable Portuguese maid, a casual guest who, like the character in the play *The Man Who*

Came to Dinner, had simply stayed on, a beautiful chatelaine and a husband who often went to bed at six p.m.

"You were going to tell me about all the other amenities," she said, gently.

"Oh, yes." Caroline sat down and handed her a leaflet which she had tucked into the back pocket of her jeans. "Chancy did this," she explained. "We're getting some larger ones printed for the Tourist Board. It's quite attractive, don't you think?"

Jessica saw an extremely well-executed picture of King's Folly, with lines radiating outwards pointing to smaller insets: a girl on a horse, someone playing tennis, a man fishing in what she took to be the disused gravel pits, another bathing in the sea, a youth walking with a backpack, a stately home and, finally, at the bottom, a woman sitting at an easel painting.

"Chancy's quite an artist," Caroline explained. "He's offered to take guests who are keen on painting to some of the best sites, give them a little tuition and return later to see how they're getting on."

"How extraordinary," Jessica replied. "I actually brought my old painting things. I dabbled a little in my teens before my parents insisted, wisely as it turned out, that I took a secretarial training. Then, after I married, I forgot all about my youthful aspirations. I thought it might be an idea to take it up again now I'm . . . well, retired."

"Really? If you were here longer, I'm sure Chancy would be only too pleased . . . "

The words were out of Jessica's mouth before she could stop them. "I should very much like to stay on for a while, that is, if the Daye House is free?"

"Would you? That's fine by us. Our only bookings are for two couples wanting rooms in the farmhouse for a few nights next week. I'll tell Chancy. He'll be pleased. Say about eleven tomorrow morning? He's got so many ideas for making King's Folly more viable. This extra amenity is quite cheap," she added, almost apologetically. "I often think I'd like to take advantage of it myself only . . . well, I'm afraid there's always so much to do."

"I'm sure you have your hands full. I'm so sorry your husband isn't well."

"Oh, Leo." All at once Caroline's expression changed. She looked older, slightly apprehensive. "He's been in poor health for some time," she said, guardedly. Then she got up, adding, abruptly, "Come along, Gracie. We must be on our way." Within seconds, she was gone.

In bed that night, Jessica thought long and hard about the extraordinary set-up, especially the mysterious Leo. She tried to imagine him, but failed. Soon, the good dinner and the half bottle of wine on the house, helped her into a dreamless sleep.

In the morning, having made herself some tea with the equipment provided, she was later brought fresh rolls and coffee by a small dark beaming Mercedes.

"*Bon-dias, madame*. Bee-utiful day. You lucky. You stay, I hear."

"Yes," Jessica answered, finding herself breaking sympathetically into the same idiom. "I stay."

"Verry good, Meeses King, say you go paint. You like peek-neek, yes?"

"Yes, I like very much."

"Good, good. I go tell Meeses King. She in garden, since five o'clock."

"*Five o'clock?*"

"Oh, yes, Meeses King, she work verry hard. Mr Chancy help, but him not know much about garden."

Mercedes withdrew, still beaming.

Whatever was the matter with Leo, Jessica wondered. What was keeping him in bed? Did he ever help his wife? Or was he really ill? Some fatal disease, perhaps? No, that was morbid. Besides, Caroline looked fairly happy, at least most of the time. She did not appear to be an overburdened young wife with a dying husband. Yet Jessica could not quite forget the way she had left so suddenly the night before, once Leo's indisposition had been mentioned.

About nine thirty, Jessica decided to explore the King's Folly garden in which her hostess, by all accounts, spent so much time. She found the vegetable plot disproportionately large. Its produce could not possibly be used just by the house itself, even if the Kings were catering to full capacity. This was a veritable *market* garden, presumably another of the sidelines which went to make the establishment viable. When, a little later, she saw the station wagon draw up at the back door and Caroline coming to meet Chancy as he got out of it, her surmise was confirmed. "A most satisfactory morning," she heard him say. "Carsons and Co. took the lot and want anything else you can send. You must have started darned early this morning to have done all that picking and bunching."

Jessica could not hear her reply and was, indeed, glad that she could not. She felt somehow that she was eavesdropping on the private financial affairs of the Kings. Quickly, she made her way down to the dovecot at the end of the long grass path and entered its dark interior through an open stone archway. Here, she felt she could safely be lost for a while, until it was time to get ready for her painting expedition or tuition or whatever Chancy called it.

The voice from the corner made her heart miss a couple of beats. It was low, clear but oddly expressionless, although it said, perfectly politely, "Good morning. Forgive me. I'm afraid I have startled you."

Coming straight from strong sunlight into practically complete darkness, she could not at first even see its owner. Then, as her eyes grew accustomed to the gloom, she saw a man rising from a chair, a large, oldish, bear of a man with a pale face. Rather as the light began slowly infiltrating the dovecot, so did the realisation dawn on her that this was Leo. Hastily, she too apologised.

"I'm sorry," she said. "I was exploring your splendid garden. I'm staying at The Daye House."

"Yes," he replied. "I know."

She saw that the chair on which she thought he had been sitting was actually a camp bed, and that there was a tray with a thermos and a mug on the floor beside it. Possibly aware of the need for a little further explanation, he went on, "I sleep here sometimes at this time of year . . . when I'm having a bad patch. I find the doves are much gentler alarm clocks than the birds in the eaves round the house. Summer isn't exactly helpful to insomniacs. Although I did quite well this morning."

Did you, Jessica found herself thinking, angrily. Did you sleep on while your wife was bent double picking all the stuff for Carsons and Co.? Or did you just skulk in the dovecot pretending not to notice? And where, for that matter, had Chancy been? Couldn't he have come and lent a hand? She made a point of looking at her watch.

"I must go," she said, quietly. "I'm having a painting lesson soon."

"Ah, yes. I'm sure you will find that most agreeable."

Baffled, she went back into the sunlight.

4

"I DARE say you'd like to take your own car," Chancy said, as he handed her a picnic shortly before eleven o'clock. "I mean, you don't exactly want to be left stranded with no means of a getaway."

"Well, no. I hadn't actually thought that far."

"I'll go ahead in my old banger, then. Leave you to follow. Perhaps I ought just to check your painting equipment first."

"Thank you. Please do, although I think I've got all I require. I decided perhaps today I'd concentrate on sketching. Get my hand in, so to speak."

"Good idea."

They set off in convoy, bumping over the rough track she had taken the previous evening, before veering right along an even rougher track until they reached another gate. Chancy stopped, opened and shut it for both of them and then, a little further on they came to the edge

41

of what seemed like some precipice. She pulled up beside him. Ahead lay an expanse of England so beautiful that she somehow felt ashamed, at her age, never to have seen it before. Blues, greens and splashes of yellow melted into a hazy limitless distance.

"It's quite a view, isn't it?" he said, as they got out of their respective cars and stood looking at it. "But I think it's a bit too vast to tackle as a start." He pointed out the various landmarks, even a glimpse of the Bristol Channel away to their right.

She remained silent, taking it all in, thinking what a limited life she had led. It was all very well not to be keen on going abroad, but never to have taken the trouble to explore her native country seemed downright criminal.

Presently Chancy said, "There's a small village about three miles away. Some people call it chocolate boxy. You know, there's an old Norman church with a lych gate and it even has a village shop, although the government seems hell bent on eliminating them. I find that the few visitors I've escorted there have rather enjoyed setting up an easel on the green. Believe it or not, they actually play cricket on it at weekends. There's also a handy pub called the Whistling Pig instead of the usual Pig and Whistle, in case you find yourself in need of any alcoholic refreshment. I've got to go into Wells to get some garden stuff for Caro. Suppose I come back around two thirty and see how you're getting on?"

"That sounds splendid."

She found Chancy's choice of site all that he had proclaimed it to be. Seated under a large oak tree, she felt she could well have just stayed there or simply wandered around the village, idling the morning away. But, mindful that she would have to have something to show him when he returned, after a brief tour she decided to make a start on the church. Soon, she became aware that her presence was attracting the attention of some of the younger generation. They stood in a group, a little distance behind her, and then one or another of them began drawing nearer before backing away giggling, rather like a game of grandmother's steps. She did not mind.

After all, she thought to herself, I *am* a grandmother and they remind me of Jason when he was young. She made a mental note to telephone Marianne that evening and tell her where she had fetched up.

Meanwhile, she sat on her camp stool, taking her time, feeling more relaxed than she had done in years, congratulating herself that miraculously, at least for the moment, she seemed to have found all she was looking for. At one o'clock she broke off sketching and went to collect her picnic from the car. It was, as expected, exactly right: a slice of quiche, salad, a small carton of gooseberry fool, cheese and biscuits and a bottle of Perrier in a cold container. She supposed she could have gone over to the Whistling Pig and bought some cider, but she felt in no need of the alcoholic refreshment which Chancy had suggested. Afterwards, she stretched out on the grass and almost went to sleep but, half an hour later found her back at her easel, determined to produce some kind of reasonable sketch for him to criticise.

The children seemed to have disappeared

now but, suddenly, a deep West Country voice behind her made her jump. She turned quickly, certain that she had heard it before. The man must have crept up on her and was now standing uncomfortably close, the same big uncouth man at the Tourist Board who had directed her, albeit with great reluctance, to King's Folly the previous evening.

"Found it all right, then," he said, looking more unattractive than ever, his shirt open wide revealing a hirsute chest, his beer belly protruding over a pair of dirty old flannel trousers. She was so surprised to see him that all she could reply was, simply, "Yes." She did not add thank you and wished devoutly that he would go away. What on earth was he doing? Why wasn't he at the Tourist Board, attempting to deflect other tourists from going anywhere near King's Folly?

"I see Chancy's got you on to thic drawin' caper," he went on, glancing briefly at her easel and ignoring her obvious desire to be left alone.

"No," she answered, stiffly. "I always intended to do some painting while on holiday. It was just fortunate that I seem to have found such an ideal place to stay."

"You're not moving on, then?"

His inquisitiveness irked her. There was something insolent and far too friendly in his manner.

"No," was all she said again, and turned back deliberately to her sketching. Then, to her relief, she noticed Chancy's car approaching. By the time it pulled up, her unwelcome acquaintance had completely vanished.

Chancy was encouraging when he saw what she had accomplished, but not overfulsome in his praise, for which she was grateful. She appreciated having a serious critic. He put her right on one or two points of perspective, suggested that there should be more sky and less foreground and asked where she had first studied art and whether she had ever regretted giving it up. He sat on the grass beside her, saying that he himself wished he had applied himself more, like his sister, Kate, who lived in the United States and had made a name for herself as a portrait painter. He himself had apparently gone to Paris to study on leaving school and then on to Italy, remaining for a time in Siena. Back in London, he had even had one or two exhibitions. "Friends were kind," he said. "Several pictures sold. But then, I don't know, I hadn't got Kate's dedication. I chucked it all in. I wanted an open-air life. Through one of my friends I heard about Leo and Caro who had decided to get out of the rat race and go in for farming. Apparently things weren't working out quite as they'd hoped and they were taking paying guests. This friend gave me their address and, on the spur of the moment, I bought a caravan and decided to look them up. That was some three or four years ago and, as you can see, I'm still here."

"Did you know their dairyman, well, ex-dairyman, that is?"

"Not very well." He seemed surprised. "Of course, by the time I came on the scene they'd given up cows. But why do you ask?"

"Because just before you arrived a little while ago, he was standing right behind me."

Chancy frowned. "Really? I know he lives in the village but I never noticed anyone skedaddle. How the hell did you know it was him?"

"Because we met at the Tourist Board last night. He gave me directions as to how to get to King's Folly, only he didn't seem at all keen on my going there."

"Oh, he wouldn't be. He's really got it in for Leo and Caro, although I'm sure they gave him the proper redundancy pay-out and all that. His name's Bill Shergold, but he doesn't work for the Tourist Board. I understand he's never done another hand's turn since he left King's Folly. He and his wife have parted company and he now lives with his married daughter. I believe she works at the Board. I expect he just called in there to cadge some cash off her for a booze-up."

"I see. It seems a pity from the Kings' point of view if he goes there often and tries to put people off becoming their paying guests. He must do them out of quite a bit of business. I hope his daughter doesn't take the same attitude."

"Edna Yates? Shouldn't think so. She's

a nice girl, by all accounts. Her husband, Sidney, works at Carsons, the firm that takes all our garden produce. Anyway, I'm sure now Leo and Caro are getting so much more established in that line, as well as taking in paying guests, they can afford to ignore Bill Shergold. As a matter of fact, Caro's dead keen on turning King's Folly into a real hotel. She's immensely capable. If only . . . "

He stopped abruptly and stood up. Jessica began packing away her paraphernalia. She suspected that Chancy had checked himself just in time before saying something which might have been construed as disloyal concerning the present owner of King's Folly.

5

SHE did not meet Leo again for five days, days which passed so quickly and pleasantly that she could scarcely believe she had been at King's Folly a week. Other guests had come and gone, but Caroline assured her that the Daye House accommodation was still free.

"I'm sort of fixed," she told Marianne, on the telephone. "It's so nice here. I don't think I'll move on, at least not for a while. The owners are . . . well, it's difficult to describe them. They're unusual. The wife is charming and there's an artist chap who lives in a caravan in the grounds who's helping me to take up painting again."

"Ma sounds as if she's struck lucky," her daughter-in-law said to her second husband, Terence, after another call from Jessica. He was a widower, a retired naval officer, who liked and had accepted that his new wife's one-time mother-in-law was now part of his own family. He approved of Jessica and she approved of him. Having, much to his regret, had no children during his first marriage, he was proving to be an excellent stepfather to Jason, who was now backpacking with a friend round Europe. Jessica hoped and prayed that all would be well with them. Through force of circumstances, she had become so involved in her grandson's early upbringing that she found it hard to let go. Although she had never felt too happy about the use of the modern expression 'bonding', she knew that she had bonded with Jason far better than she had ever done with Simon, her own son. Jason would always come first and foremost in her life.

Sometimes, Jessica wished she had had more grandchildren, for she realised that she had all her eggs in one basket. She felt it must be sad to reach one's allotted span in life with no stake, as it were, in the younger generation. She wondered whether Caro and Leo were childless through choice or had been denied the choice. At least, she imagined they had no children, for Caro would surely have mentioned it if they had. She would have made such an excellent mother, Jessica thought, and supposed that was probably why all her abundant energy was now directed into other channels. She hoped her hostess wasn't overdoing things and wondered whether she might offer to help, if only with the watering of an evening. Most of it seemed to be done by automatic sprinklers, but she had noticed Caroline often wielded a hose or used a can on the more inaccessible parts. Jessica felt it was high time she had a talk with her, because she was concerned about monopolising the Daye House without paying more. She sensed that Caroline liked having her there — they were on Christian name terms by now — but if some family suddenly wanted the accommodation, it didn't seem right that Caroline might refuse them.

It was with these thoughts in mind, she decided to wheel her own dinner trolley over to the house that night and seek out her hostess. The back door was open and she pushed it inside the kitchen. No one seemed to be about except Gracie, who wagged her tail enthusiastically, confirming Caroline's remark that she doubted she was much of a guard dog. Supposing that her hostess was in the vegetable garden, Jessica made her way there, Gracie at her heels. The day had been heavy with heat and the pansies in the two tubs on either side of the small gate which led to it were beginning to wilt.

Then she saw him: Leo. He was stripped to the waist, wielding a hosepipe. There was something curiously majestic about him, almost as if he might have been a statue which occasionally came to life. She watched him stoop, remove one of the sprinklers to another position and then go back to his hand watering. She wondered where Caroline was, what Chancy was doing, whether Leo would remember her as the guest who had disturbed his early morning a little while ago.

Hesitantly, she waited, while Gracie flopped down beside her. Then, as Leo moved closer, he suddenly seemed to become aware of her existence, raised his left hand and said "Good evening", in a way which did not appear to require any acknowledgement.

"Good evening," she replied, fearing that this was perhaps the end of their brief encounter. Leo King, intent on his watering, did not seem to wish for any closer contact with his guest. Jessica felt somehow insulted, intimidated, an interloper. How could he hope to attract tourists if this was the way he treated them, while his poor wife obviously did her best to be so hospitable. Why, he was almost as bad as Bill Shergold. What *was* the matter with Caroline's husband? She supposed it must be some mental trouble and she should, perhaps, make allowances. At least she had found him *working*. She was about to retreat, since it seemed the only option left to her when, much to her surprise, he remarked, "I trust you are enjoying the Folly." She felt that there could almost be a double meaning in the way he simply referred to 'the Folly' instead of 'King's Folly'. Then she rejected her idea as fanciful. The name was occasionally shortened, even by Chancy.

"Very much," she replied. "Your wife

has made me most welcome. Her cooking is . . . out of this world." She felt she could have made a less banal observation, said something more original, but Leo actually smiled.

"Caro," he said, bending again to move the sprinkler to a row of carrots, "used to do directors' luncheons in the City when I first met her. She was much sought after."

"I'm not surprised." Again Jessica felt his words could well have had a double meaning. She was sure Caroline was sought after, but not only for her cooking. She hoped she could keep this man talking since, albeit inadvertently, he had made an interesting revelation as to how he had met his future wife.

There was a sudden clap of thunder in the distance. He looked up. "Could be I'm wasting my time," he remarked. "It seems as if we're in for a storm. They're sometimes rather bad up here." Even as he spoke, a few drops of rain had begun to fall. "You'd best get back to the Daye." It was said quite kindly but she felt as if she were being dismissed.

It was, indeed, not only a bad storm

but a frightening one. Yet it was not just the thunder and lightning which kept her awake. Where on earth was Caro? And Chancy? Could they possibly have been out on the loose together? It was well past eleven when she heard the sound of a car returning, indistinct voices, doors opening and shutting. Later still, she kept thinking that Leo's remark about wasting his time had been all too correct. The rain had been torrential.

She was surprised when Caroline appeared with her picnic the next morning. "Chancy," she explained, "has to lie low for a few days. I had to take him to the hospital last night. He cut his hand on the rotary hoe and it was a bit more than Dr Pinnegar, our local GP, could cope with."

"I'm terribly sorry."

"Oh, he'll be all right. He's already had an anti-tetanus jab and all that but . . . well, he's not quite as handy with machinery as he is with a paint brush. Incidentally, thank you very much for bringing back your dinner trolley last night. You shouldn't have bothered."

"It was nothing. As a matter of fact,

I came to ask you if I could help in any way, perhaps with the watering, but your husband seemed to be attending to that."

"How good of you, but you're a guest, a *paying* guest. You're meant to be on holiday. Besides, Leo is on the up again, thank goodness."

"He's been rather ill, I take it?" Jessica could not help questioning her this time.

The same look which she had noticed the first evening when Leo's name had cropped up now came into Caroline's eyes. "Well, yes. He hasn't been well off and on for quite a while. We bought King's Folly knowing nothing about farming. We were fools, really, and came a cropper. Chancy's probably told you."

"Only a little. Not about your husband's illness." Jessica felt that Bill Shergold had almost told her more, at least about the failure of the enterprise, but that it might be better not to mention it.

"Leo became terribly depressed," Caroline went on. "That's been far worse than losing so much money. Do you know anything about depression?"

"No. Not really."

"It's a heller. Leo's been on pills for ages. The doctors say they help, but I have reservations. He's not allowed to drive while he's taking medication. Chancy or I have to ferry him about and that makes him more depressed. Personally, I think that the only thing that would help would be to make some money, kickstart the King's Folly economy, as they say, see everything pick up again. Leo hates being defeated. He couldn't possibly go back to being a city slicker. That's why we sold off some land, put a bit into set-aside and just kept a few grazing stock, although now they're up for auction. I'm pinning my hopes on the catering venture and the market garden. At least that seems to be paying off at last. In spite of the recession, I'm sure we'll make out in the end."

"I'm so glad," Jessica said. But it's *you* who are doing the making out she thought, privately, as Caroline continued, "Chancy, of course, was heaven sent. He's lived up to his nickname in the nicest possible way. I can't think what we'd have done without him. He arrived at the psychological moment and stayed on to help, just for the sheer love of it."

Again Jessica thought: for the love of you, perhaps? She remembered he had said he wanted an open-air life, that he hadn't sufficient dedication to apply himself to his art. She had thought of him as something of a wanderer, unable to settle down, but he had settled all right at King's Folly. Finding himself in the presence of this devastatingly beautiful woman in need of male support could well have been irresistible. A damsel in distress rescued by a most attractive knight. But what about Leo, the unfortunate third in the eternal triangle. Jessica supposed that the poor wretched man had been more or less obliged to accept the situation for expediency's sake. Her knowledge of the world was curiously limited, but she was aware that many a man who loved his wife accepted her infidelity when there seemed no other choice. Rather than lose Caroline, lose King's Folly, Leo had chosen forbearance — although at what a cost. He may have been depressed when Chancy came on the scene, but the subsequent situation, despite the much-needed support both man and wife derived from their unusual guest, could hardly have helped him from the emotional point of view.

Jessica felt that she herself was rather like Chancy, in that she had arrived out of the blue and wanted to stay. Perhaps the place had some strange kind of magnetism about it. But whatever it was, she was determined not to add to anyone's problems. "Look," she said to Caroline. "I like it here. I should love to book in for at least a month. But I absolutely insist on paying more for the Daye House than what I'm doing now. Besides, it could be that some of my family might like to spend a little time with me."

6

MARIANNE and Terence came down to spend a few days at King's Folly the following week. Jessica was delighted to hear the latest news of Jason and they, in turn, were delighted to find her enjoying her new environment so much. Marianne thought Caroline could have been a model, Chancy an impresario, Mercedes, with her broken English, a comic turn and the brooding Leo a kind of Heathcliff character. "Substitute Wuthering Heights for King's Folly," she said, "and you have the most intriguing scenario."

"But you haven't met the really sinister one," Jessica replied. "There's a chap called Bill Shergold who was employed by the Kings when they first came here. He was made redundant when they opted out of dairying. He's never been able to forget it."

"How on earth did you come across him?" Terence asked.

"Quite accidentally. He happened to have called in at the local Tourist Board when I first went there. He tried to put me off coming here."

"Hurt but harmless, perhaps," Marianne broke in.

"Certainly hurt, but not altogether harmless," Jessica answered.

"But if he doesn't actually work at the Tourist Board, he can't be all that much of a problem, can he? After all, he didn't put *you* off coming to King's Folly."

"No," Jessica admitted. "And I'm so glad he didn't."

On the last night of their visit, Terence suggested that they went out for an evening meal and his invitation extended to all the occupants of King's Folly. There were no other guests staying and Terence said it would do Caroline good to have a break from cooking. She was hesitant of accepting and Jessica could see it was difficult for her. Leo would certainly not want to come and it would hardly seem right for both her and Chancy to go off enjoying themselves while leaving him alone. In the event, Chancy tactfully settled the matter by saying that, since his accident there were several jobs he needed to catch up on.

"Sensible chap," remarked Marianne, before they set off. "He couldn't very well do otherwise."

And when Caroline came out of the house wearing, for once, a particularly becoming dress, rather than jeans, with her long blonde hair hanging loose over her shoulders, Jessica wondered, not for the first time, whether it would be better now for Chancy to make other excuses for absenting himself from King's Folly altogether.

They dined at a new hotel called Chandlers, which Caroline was interested in, from the point of view of possibly one day extending her own enterprise. It was pleasant, the cooking was good, but the whole set-up was somehow impersonal. It had none of the individuality of King's Folly.

On their way back, they drove through the village where Jessica had executed her first picture and Terence drew up near the Whistling Pig. None of them wanted a drink, but the evening was warm and the village green cool and inviting, the customers from the inn spilling out on to it in twos and threes. The whole scene was enhanced by an air of conviviality and they got out of the car to sit under the same tree where Jessica had perched on her little camp stool during the first morning of her holiday.

Suddenly there was discord. A man staggered out of the Whistling Pig, shouting and swearing at the landlord who was obviously trying to evict him. He began weaving his way towards them and, to her dismay, Jessica realised it was Bill Shergold, although she felt that in the state he was in it was hardly likely he would recognise anybody.

But here she was wrong. A few feet from where they were sitting, he stopped, put out a hand on one of the open car doors to steady himself and said, "Why, if it ishn't li'l Mrs King o' the Cashel, havin' a nighst li'l party without her husband."

They did their best to ignore him. The fact that Bill Shergold had somehow settled himself half in and half out of their car made it difficult to make a dignified getaway. Caroline, angry and acutely embarrassed, looked away.

"Makin' any money out o' thic Dairy yet?" Bill went on, leering at them all. "Milkin' guests instead o' them Jerseys I sweated me guts on? I'm shurprised Chancy ain't here to keep an eye on you. Let you off the hook for a change, has he?"

Jessica saw that Caroline was near to tears and she herself could almost have wept with relief when a young couple bore down on them and she heard the woman say, "Come along now, Father. Time you were going home." Her husband, obviously used to extricating his father-in-law from unfortunate situations heaved Bill Shergold out of the car and, with surprising dexterity and no further words from the drunken dairyman, they manhandled him across the green, presumably in the direction of their home.

It was a distressing end to what had been, until then, an exceptionally happy evening. In the car going back to King's Folly, Caroline sat silently beside Terence, while Marianne and Jessica made desultory conversation in the back.

"I am so terribly sorry about what happened," she said, as she wished them goodnight. "Thank you so much for your . . . forbearance . . . for everything." Then she turned away quickly and almost ran into the house.

Once inside the Daye, they did not go to bed, but sat in the small sitting-room looking out on to the gathering dusk. A moon had risen and King's Folly looked strangely ephemeral, no longer the solid old farmstead it appeared to be in the daytime. Somewhere in the trees an owl hooted and Jessica felt unaccountably sad, even a little apprehensive, realising that tomorrow her visitors would be gone and she would be alone again.

Suddenly, Terence remarked, "You still intend to stay here some time, do you, Ma?"

She was surprised at his question. She thought she had made that plain. She was even more surprised when he went on, "I agree the place is a most unusual find, but I'm beginning to wonder whether it might not be better, after all, if you moved on to a more conventional set-up."

"But why, Terence?" Jessica felt that Marianne had also been taken by surprise.

"I don't know," he answered. "I dare say it's all right, but personally I'd feel happier if you weren't stuck out here in the back of beyond."

"But I have a car," she said, a little defensively. "I'm not exactly stuck."

Yet even as she spoke, she could not help thinking that the episode earlier in the evening had cast a shadow, sown doubts, shattered the idyll, in fact. Then her habitual common sense reasserted itself. Bill Shergold might be loud mouthed and too fond of his drink, but he couldn't *really* do any harm. Although, as she lay awake, for once tossing and turning, she wasn't quite so sure. She certainly didn't like the way he had insinuated a relationship between Caroline and Chancy, one which she herself suspected but would never go as far as to voice, even to Terence and Marianne. It was none of her business and, to all intents and purposes, they behaved with admirable discretion.

It was Marianne who, having made

a pot of tea for them all the following morning, came and sat on her bed and surprised her still further. "I hope," she said, "Terence didn't upset you last night."

"Why, no," Jessica lied. "It's nice of him to be so concerned about me. I suppose he thinks I'm a bit on the old side to be . . . well, mixed up with the somewhat strange lifestyles of younger people whom I hardly know."

Marianne put down her cup and stared out of the window. "If you're referring to the Caroline/Chancy situation, it isn't that which Terence worries about, I mean, nice as he is, Chancy doesn't strike us as being exactly a ladies man."

7

HOW stupid could one get, Jessica thought, after she had waved Marianne and Terence goodbye. Why on earth had it not crossed her mind? *Of course*, there was no eternal triangle. In any case, Caroline would never have been so heartless as to carry on with another man under the nose of her sick husband. Jessica wondered how she could ever have entertained the idea. A lot seemed to fall into place now. Leo might be irked and jealous that he was so dependent on a younger man's help. He might even resent Chancy's undoubted charisma and affability with all and sundry, but he was astute enough to realise — as she herself had been obtuse enough not to realise — that he had no fear of being cuckolded or losing a wife who, when all was said and done, worked so loyally on behalf of him and King's Folly.

Yet Terence's suggestion that Jessica

should move on, still puzzled her. Marianne had not enlarged on it and Terence had carefully refrained from making any more reference to the idea before leaving that morning.

Feeling unsettled and disinclined to paint that day, Jessica, equipped with the customary picnic, decided to take herself off to the stately home depicted in Chancy's leaflet. Here, she joined a group being shown round by a good-looking middle-aged woman, who seemed to have the whole history of the place so word perfect it was as if she had a tape recorder in her head. Yet she also appeared able to answer any question put to her with an off-the-cuff expertise which, while briefly satisfying the questioner, somehow prohibited further enquiries. With her obviously dyed coiffure matching her smart yellow shirtwaister, there was something slightly intimidating about her.

"No," she would say, "The Earl and Countess do not actually live here any more", or "Yes, the library is said to be one of the best in England. The present earl's father was a great bibliophile and did his utmost to preserve the books in such a splendid condition."

Jessica wondered whether her late employer, Gerald Frobisher, had ever seen them and what he would have thought if he had. They were certainly an impressive sight. Row upon row of leather-bound tomes from floor to ceiling, secured from the public by a rope barrier. So interested did she become, that the security guard was obliged to hurry her along a little in order to catch up with the group of sightseers who were now about to have a dissertation on some portraits in the long gallery.

"No, Queen Elizabeth did not sleep here," she heard their guide continue, "but it is said that Charles II, whose picture we are looking at, sought refuge in these parts. It is only hearsay, but it is thought that King's Folly, a farmstead some ten miles away, then owned by staunch royalists, once accommodated him for the night."

"Gee, fancy that!" came a loud American voice from a man standing just in front of Jessica. "Why is it called a Folly?"

For the first time, the lady guide seemed a little disconcerted. "I'm not sure," she replied, coldly, and then, her confidence returning, she went on, "Follies were usually architectural extravaganzas, but King's Folly is said to be a splendid example of a seventeenth century manorial dwelling. Perhaps it was foolish of the King to shelter there." She appeared to feel that this little impromptu observation was the end of the matter.

"But if he wasn't caught," persisted the fat American, who was wearing white shorts and a bright red shirt, "then the King probably made a cute move."

"Maybe."

Jessica now began to feel rather sorry for the guide. She wore no wedding ring and she imagined her, going home alone, exhausted after being on her feet all day, repeating the same information over and over again, as she conducted a whole lot of rubbernecks through the stately rooms. Jessica felt even sorrier for her when the American went on, "We don't have Follies where I come from. Is this one public?"

"I believe," came the reply, "the

present owners run it as some kind of guest house."

"Gee. That's great!" He turned to his wife, an equally large figure wearing even brighter attire: a trouser suit in every colour of the rainbow. "Suppose we try and make a stopover there tonight, honey?"

Although Jessica did not take to the man, she felt it was almost incumbent on her to procure for Caroline any custom which might come her way. "I happen to be staying at King's Folly at the moment," she said to him, quietly. "I can give you the address if you like."

"Why, you don't say! Isn't that just the ticket? Frank and Milly Merton from Idaho. Pleased to meet you, ma'am. Do you think they'd have a room?" Both he and his wife held out their hands and shook Jessica's vigorously.

"So far as I know. You would need to telephone, of course."

"Sure. I'm much obliged, ma'am."

Jessica wrote down her own name and that of the Kings, together with their address and telephone number. She wondered whether the plumbing in the

73

house itself would be up to the Mertons' standard, but from what she had seen of all Caroline's improvements she felt they might be pleasantly surprised, especially as they were obviously keen on seeing 'as much of the old country as possible', as Frank remarked, on parting. Later that evening, when Jessica saw a huge Cadillac nosing its way along the uneven track, she supposed that the least she could do would be to ask them over to the Daye House after dinner.

They arrived at her door about nine thirty bearing, much to Jessica's surprise and embarrassment, a bottle of Napoleon brandy and three glasses which they had borrowed from Caroline. "One good turn deserves another," Frank said, beginning to pour out lavish measures. "We shouldn't be here but for you. But, my, aren't we glad we came."

Dressed now in less garish outfits, they seemed a great deal nicer. Jessica had thought of them as typical brash tourists but, after only a short while, she realised that there was far more to them than that. Frank turned out to be a retired lawyer, his wife a former nurse. "I was over here in the war," he said, "but somehow I never got to these parts. After I was demobbed I took a legal training and then, when Milly and I married I promised her that one day we'd visit the old country but, somehow, what with the kids coming along and everything, we've only just made it. This Folly sure is a surprise. And little Mrs King, why she's just adorable."

"And a wunnderful cook," added Milly, obviously amused and well used to her husband's eye for a pretty woman. "I sure would like to pack her in my bag on our return trip."

"But I dare say Mr King would have something to say about that," Frank broke in.

It occurred to Jessica that Frank had possibly made the same mistake as she had in the beginning, for she had seen Chancy helping Caroline in the kitchen quarters that evening. But here she was wrong. "He's the big guy, isn't he?" Frank went on. "Kinda withdrawn, quiet. I guess his wife spreads enough cheer for both of them, though. You staying long?"

"Another two weeks or so."

"Too bad we can't stop on . . . but, well, our itinerary keeps us on the move. This King's Folly is what I believe you'd call a one-off. Can't help thinking it must be a bit lonely here when the fall comes along. I don't suppose the Kings get much custom then."

"No, I suppose not."

After the Mertons left next day, Jessica kept thinking about Frank's last remark. King's Folly would certainly be very different in a month or so's time. Even now, it had begun to get dark a little earlier each day. The nights were drawing in. Few strangers would want to brave the steep ascent and the rough track to the house once summer had ended. Unless there was better access, Caroline's idea of extending her establishment was really so much pie in the sky. It was sad to think that perhaps it might go the same way as all the other enterprises the Kings had unfortunately gone in for in an effort to keep their heads above water.

Jessica tried to visualise them later on: Leo, Caroline and Chancy in the grip of bleak midwinter while Mercedes, sensible woman, had flown off to her warmer native clime. She, Jessica, would think of King's Folly while tucked up in her centrally-heated London flat, would even think about Frank and Milly Merton who she was sure would be equally well insulated against the elements in faraway Idaho, except that she had absolutely no idea what winter was actually like there.

But even as she gave way to such surmises, at the back of her mind, Jessica knew that there was something much more important that she ought to be thinking about now: what she had come away to do, the reason for her holiday. She was meant to be making plans for her own future, instead of allowing herself to become caught up in the complexity of other people's present.

8

SOON after the Mertons' departure, Jessica was woken in the middle of the night by the sound of a door banging and hurrying footsteps. She got up, lifted a corner of the curtains and peered out. In the light of a full moon, she could see Caroline running towards Chancy's caravan.

A little while earlier, she might have suspected the worst. Now, whatever was happening seemed to take on another, more disturbing, connotation. Something urgent, some catastrophe, must have happened. Was it to do with Leo? Did Caroline need help? She waited, uneasily.

Presently, Caroline returned and then came the sound of Chancy's old car starting up. Was he going for a doctor? Should she go across to the house? Jessica was well aware that she had become more than just a guest, and yet . . .

She looked towards King's Folly. It was

now in total darkness again. Lights which had been switched on had been switched off. In that case, Jessica supposed that she should go back to bed. But she slept fitfully. Shortly before seven, although somewhat later than usual, she was relieved to hear the station wagon drive off with produce from the market garden.

When Mercedes brought Jessica's breakfast, she volunteered, with barely suppressed excitement, the information that "Mr Chancy, he gone in the night."

"Gone?"

"Yes."

Jessica hesitated. It was not really for her to question Mercedes as to the goings-on of her employers, much as she wanted to know what had happened. But she soon found she had no need to probe. Mercedes, obviously relishing her role as reporter of the drama, went on, "Mr Chancy, he go America."

"*America?*"

"Yes. Sister very ill. Car crash. Beeg car crash. Shall I make you peek-neek? Mrs King gone Carsons with *vegetais*. Not back yet."

"Oh, no. No, thank you. Please don't bother." In the circumstances, the last thing Jessica wanted was to feel she was causing any extra trouble. "I'll be going out to lunch," she added, rather lamely.

But would she? After Mercedes had reluctantly withdrawn, Jessica thought that the least she could do would be to offer some practical help. When she heard the sound of the station wagon returning, she went across to the kitchen quarters, where she found Caroline sitting on the floor with her arms round Gracie. For the first time since Jessica had known her, she seemed utterly defeated.

"I came," Jessica said, "to see if there was anything I could do."

Caroline stared at her. "You've heard, then?"

"Yes. Mercedes told me."

"You're very kind but . . . I don't know. I mean, I can't quite think what . . . will happen now."

"Leo?" Jessica ventured.

"He doesn't know yet. He was having one of his bad nights."

Jessica could feel her anger rising. She

supposed the wretched man must have been down in the dovecot, where she had first encountered him. Then, gradually, her natural compassion took over. She must only think about Caroline. The girl was so courageous, but so young, so vulnerable to cope alone, with a sick husband, a shaky business and now suddenly deprived of her mainstay. How on earth would she be able to carry on at King's Folly without Chancy? The prospect looked bleak.

"You can't have had much sleep yourself," Jessica said. "Suppose you go upstairs and lie down. Mercedes and I can manage. Have you any bookings?"

"No, thank goodness. At least, not until the weekend. Oh God, I never thought I'd be pleased about that. But you're a *guest*," she added quickly, with a touch of her usual conscientiousness.

"And a friend, too, I hope," Jessica replied. "I shan't want any meals for the time being. We'll talk later."

Caroline gave in. Near to tears and with an almost inaudible thank you, she disappeared upstairs, Gracie following.

For a moment or two Jessica waited,

wondering about her next move. Then there was a sound at the doorway and she turned to see Leo standing there, the expression on his face quite blank. She wanted to rush at him, shake him into life, make him aware of his responsibilities. Instead, she said, "I'm afraid there's been bad news. Chancy's had to fly to America. His sister has met with a car accident."

Leo passed a hand over his face, rather like a child, wanting to hide from unpleasantness. Then he asked, "Where is Caro?"

"I suggested she went back to bed. She must have had a terrible night and she's been up early working in the garden and taking the stuff to Carsons."

"I see." Without another word, he went through into the hall and she heard him mounting the stairs.

Sheer frustration took hold of her now. How to help? Where to start? Outside, it had started to rain. Presumably that would take care of the watering for a while. With no visitors until the weekend, there would be no one extra to cater for, particularly if she took herself off for the day. Perhaps it *would* be better if she went away altogether, as Terence had intimated. After all, she had not known the Kings or King's Folly and its strange set-up until a few weeks ago. The absence of Chancy might be a blessing in disguise, galvanise Leo into action, cure him, in fact. She knew so little about depression. Though usually a tolerant person, this man's illness engendered an extraordinary intolerance in her.

Suddenly, Mercedes appeared in the kitchen, and went over to the sink, where she started to peel some vegetables. "I make *Batatas*. Beeg *Batatas*. Do for tonight and tomorrow. Last long time. Are you sure you not want peek-neek?"

"Yes. Quite sure, thank you. In fact, please will you tell Mrs King I shall be out to dinner also." As soon as she had said this, Jessica realised her mistake, Mercedes was obviously hurt.

"You not like my *Batatas*? Is very good. Portuguese special."

Jessica did her best to make amends. "I'm sure it is, Mercedes. But maybe I could have it tomorrow? You said it lasts a long time."

"Oh, yes. Nice long time." Mercedes

smiled again, apparently satisfied.

Jessica went back to the Daye. Until she could have a long talk with Caroline, she felt that it was perhaps best to remove herself, at least for a while. Man and wife were together. Mercedes seemed to be coping admirably. The rain was taking care of the garden. Within half an hour, she drove off down the track.

She was late getting back that night. She had not meant to go so far and was surprised when she found herself so close to the Bristol Channel. She bought a sandwich and a carton of orange juice from a roadside café and drove on down to a small bay, where she sat in her car, eating and thinking. Later on, after finishing what she knew Mercedes would have considered a very poor 'peek-neek', she took herself off for a walk along the shore, despite the poor weather. The sensible side of her nature told her that there was no doubt Terence had been agonisingly right. She had always known he had great perception and had quickly recognised one of her failings: a need to be needed. In some uncanny way, he had foreseen she might become too involved in the King's Folly establishment, which was neither conventional nor viable. She sensed the way his mind would have worked, helped by some background details supplied by Marianne. Here was his new mother-in-law, used to being exploited by her late husband, her son and her employer, Gerald Frobisher and, up to a point, by her grandson, when he was younger, even though that had probably been a labour of love. Jessica could imagine Terence and Marianne discussing her present position, the two of them wishing she had gone on some well-organised cruise.

She was still nowhere near the answer to the predicament in which she now found herself, when she drove back to King's Folly much later than she had intended. On her return journey she had stopped briefly, at the Whistling Pig, knowing they did takeaway suppers, but by the time she left it was getting quite dark.

Once she had negotiated the gate and started along the uneven track, she could see the lights in the house, but the Daye was naturally shrouded in darkness. It was only fleeting, so fleeting in fact, that she wondered whether she had imagined it, but as she drew nearer she thought she saw a figure move quickly away from outside her bedroom window.

9

JESSICA was delighted when Marianne rang up to say that Jason would like to spend a day or two with her the following week. It was good to know that he was safely home and looking forward to going up to Oxford. It was also good to feel that he wanted to see his grandmother. Now that he had left school, she realised that, inevitably, his horizons would widen and his time be taken up with other activities; but she had always hoped that the bond which had been forged between them when he was young would remain. With his latest request, this looked like being the case.

She had had a long talk with Caroline the day after her trip to the sea although, having persuaded herself it had been a flight of fancy, she said nothing about seeing any figure outside the Daye House on her return. She agreed that she would stay on for another few weeks and lend a hand wherever she could until they learned more about Chancy's plans. At the moment, except for a brief transatlantic telephone call, they knew little and Jessica sensed that her presence at King's Folly gave the younger woman a kind of emotional, if transient, security.

"But if you're going to be a dogsbody," Caroline said, "I refuse to take any more money for your keep. It's not as if the Daye House is wanted. Sometimes I wonder if it was such a good idea to convert the dairy after all, and we should probably have installed a proper kitchen instead of that minute kitchenette and let holidaymakers do their own catering. It was all rather rushed through and wasn't finished until April. We never really advertised it enough. People with families had already made plans for the summer. I've a lot to learn, I suppose," she added, with a wry smile.

Jessica replied that any financial arrangements could be settled later and thought Caroline was about to end the conversation, when she suddenly went on, "Leo likes you, you know. He's all in favour of your being here, especially now. You probably think he's malingering . . . only it isn't as easy as all that. He's had many personal problems for some time, not just to do with King's Folly."

Suddenly, as if fearing she might have said too much, she added quickly, "I'm sure he'll get well, back to his old self one of these days. One has to have patience. He used to be . . . so different, when we first came down here."

Jessica tried to imagine Leo different, enthusiastic, full of hope. She wondered what were the other problems Caroline had referred to and marvelled at her patience and perseverance. "How often does he see his doctor?" she asked.

"Oh, he sees Jack Pinnegar about once a fortnight. But he also sees a specialist in Bristol every two months or so. In fact, I'm due to drive him there this Friday only . . . "

"Only what? I'll be here. Why don't you both have a proper day out? I'm sure Mercedes and I can manage, even if you do happen to have guests. Just tell me what to do, especially in the garden. I may not be as nimble as I once was and I wouldn't say my fingers are all that green nowadays, but I used to look after quite a large garden in Scotland for many years."

Caroline stared at her. "You're sure you don't mind?"

"Of course not. I'll enjoy it."

When the time came, Jessica found herself enjoying it even more than she had anticipated. No other visitors were expected and, but for the distressing question mark — or marks — hanging over King's Folly and its inhabitants, she felt she could have been at peace, as she gardened in the warm August sunshine. I am not good at holidays, she said to herself. What I am doing now seems so very much more worth while.

With Gracie flopped down beside her and Mercedes busy indoors, she set to work, weeding, staking, picking plums and tomatoes, sweeping and trundling rubbish down to a compost heap near the dovecot. It was the time of year when, although the sun was still strong, there were signs everywhere that the best of the summer was over, that not only were the days shortening but somehow life seemed to be slowly leaving the countryside. It was a time for harvesting, tidying and gathering up the remains, for quietly preparing, as it were, for the onslaught of winter on this lonely windswept upland.

Jessica felt strangely lost towards evening when she watched Mercedes, accompanied by the faithful Gracie, set off down the track to her son's cottage. More than once she found herself looking out for the dog's return, and was inordinately pleased when she caught sight of the yellow form bounding back towards her again.

At seven, when there was still no sign of Leo and Caro, she went into the farmhouse kitchen and gave the dog her supper as instructed. Then, locking the door behind her and followed by Gracie, she trundled the trolley containing her own cold meal, prepared by Mercedes, back to the Daye House. Once inside, she poured herself a drink. The unaccustomed exercise had made her tired, but pleasantly so. She would like to have had a bath and change before sitting down to eat, but felt it would be better to wait until her host and hostess returned. They surely could not be long.

Suddenly, the sound of footsteps on the small courtyard sent her heart racing. Gracie actually gave a low growl. Jessica had not thought to lock her own front door, but now she wished she had. There was, as yet, no telephone in the Daye House, arrangements for installing a separate payphone still pending. Doing her best to remain unseen and thankful that she had not yet switched on any lights, Jessica peered out of a window, rather as she had done on the night when Caroline had gone running to Chancy's caravan.

A man, a big man, was approaching the back entrance of King's Folly. The light was fading, but she saw at a glance who it was. In fact, afterwards, Jessica realised she had instinctively known who it would be. Bill Shergold, with his hands cupped to his eyes, was peering through the kitchen window of the farmhouse.

Had he been watching the place, she wondered? He must have known Leo and Caro were out, had probably seen Mercedes leave, would know that she was alone in his precious dairy. Then, just as she moved towards her front door to try to secure it at all costs, she heard, with overwhelming relief, the distant sound of the station wagon, mercifully rescuing her from sheer panic. Long before it came into view, Bill Shergold had completely disappeared.

Jessica did not mention her unwelcome visitor to Caroline that night, nor, indeed, the next day. There seemed no point in adding to her problems. Bill Shergold was just a nuisance, she tried to tell herself. He had once looked on King's Folly and its dairy as his own domain and he was resentful at having it taken from him. He probably thought that turning his cowstalls into accommodation for holiday-makers was a sacrilege. What he had felt to be unfair dismissal had preyed on his mind until it had become an obsession, which was now forcing him to return to the scene of his ill-usage.

All the same, as Jessica continued to live up to her promise of helping out in any way she could, she was unable to rid herself of a deep feeling of unease. When he was sober, Bill Shergold could probably do no more than be awkward and unpleasant; but when he was drunk, as Jessica had witnessed him that night outside the Whistling Pig, then it could be that he might become violent. Were the inhabitants of King's Folly in any danger, especially Caroline?

If the situation had been an ordinary one, Jessica knew that she would have confided her fears to Leo. Leo would then have taken steps, particularly to protect his wife. But Leo, though having just received a not unfavourable report from his specialist, was still in no fit state to be burdened with extra worries. The person to whom Jessica felt she would automatically have spoken about the problem was Chancy; but Chancy was on the other side of the Atlantic.

There was, of course, someone in whom she thought she might confide and that was Jason. But then she rejected the idea. It would hardly be fair. It would put him in a difficult position. He probably knew that his mother and stepfather were against her staying on at King's Folly. Indeed, they might have suggested that he should try to get her to leave. She could hardly ask him not to mention her predicament to them. No, while he was with her, she would put it out of her mind. She had arranged with Caroline that for those two days she would still be, ostensibly, a guest. She and Jason would explore the district a little further. But she would take care to be back in good time each evening. She would give Jason a proper lunch at some hotel and possibly bring back a cold supper for the two of them. Fortunately, her grandson had always been an accommodating sort of boy.

10

IN the event, it was Jason who more or less forced her to bring the subject out into the open. He had arrived with some rather sophisticated photographic equipment, given to him by his mother and stepfather on the strength of his academic success. On his first evening at King's Folly he said he would like to take some 'shots in the dark'.

Jessica was slightly concerned, as she watched him disappear with all his paraphernalia shortly after nine o'clock. But she steeled herself to remember he was eighteen, would soon be away at college and if she wanted to maintain their good relationship, she would have to curb her tendency to over-protectiveness.

Nevertheless, she was glad when he arrived back at eleven, saying he had had a stroke of luck. He thought he had got a photograph of an owl taken with a telescopic lens.

"I might have got two," he told her,

"only some poacher or other messed it up."

"Poacher?"

"Well, I suppose it was a poacher. Chap moving along the hedgerow at the top of what you call Folly Bottom."

"What was he like?"

"Difficult to say. Largish. He couldn't have been a gamekeeper because he was obviously up to no good. Skedaddled pretty quickly when he saw me. Of course, he might have been having some illicit assignation with one of your country maidens. My word, Gran, this place seems full of intrigue. Better than the *Archers*. Perhaps I could get a shot of him tomorrow night if he's still hanging around."

She was silent for a while. Then she said, "I'd rather you didn't try to do that. I think I know who it was, Jason. He wasn't a poacher or a village Romeo or, for that matter, a Lady Chatterley's lover. I'm sure it would have been the man who has a grudge against the Kings."

"Grudge against the Kings? Why would anyone have a grudge against them? They're so nice. At least, the wife is.

Haven't seen much of the husband."

"This man was an employee of theirs. A dairyman who was made redundant when they sold their milking herd. Apparently, he's never been able to get over it."

"But what's he up to? I mean, what on earth was he doing prowling about like that?"

"I don't know. I don't think perhaps he knows himself. He's out of work and he drinks. I suppose he's become a bit unhinged and turned into an obsessive."

"Do they know?"

She hesitated. "They know he's conducted a kind of hate campaign against them for some time."

"But do they know he's actually casing the joint?"

"No, I don't think so."

"Well, how do *you* know, then?"

Dear God, she thought. My grandson will end up a QC. "Because I've seen him loitering about here, twice," she answered.

"And you mean you haven't told them?"

"Well, the first time I couldn't swear it was him. But the second time . . . yes.

I saw him last week when Caro and Leo were out."

"But Gran, you *must* say something. Personally, I think you should get out of here, now. So do Mum and Terence. As a matter of fact, they hoped I might be able to persuade you. You're . . . well, if you don't mind my saying so, nice but awfully gullible. You say you've been helping out because this man of all works is away and Leo is sick, but it's not right. Not right at all."

She tried to steer him away from the subject but realised, half with pride and half with hopelessness, that she was up against a determined young man with an extraordinarily logical mind.

"I'll think about it," she replied. "But I can't break a promise. I've said I'll stay on another few weeks."

"But you'll tell the Kings about what's been happening, Gran, won't you? You simply have to. You owe it to them and yourself."

"All right, Jason."

But she knew he was not satisfied. He would go home and tell Marianne and Terence exactly what was going on. It would make them more anxious than ever to get her away from King's Folly. I suppose I'm a fool, she thought. An old one, what's more, which is so much worse. What business has a grandmother, pushing seventy, to be dogsbodying in a market garden for a couple she hardly knows. I really must have a talk with Caroline, get things sorted out, possibly make a date for leaving, whether I know about Chancy's plans or not.

After Jason had gone, she asked Caroline if she would care to join her for a brandy after dinner that night. "There's still quite a bit left in the Mertons' bottle," Jessica said, "I'd like someone to help me with it. Fortunately, my grandson doesn't drink and I don't think Napoleon brandy is the sort to imbibe alone."

Caroline seemed only too pleased to accept the invitation. She arrived, accompanied by Gracie, looking tired and tense, so much so that Jessica wondered whether she should, after all, say what she intended. But she had promised Jason and when she noticed the brandy beginning to relax her guest a little, she said, "I don't quite know how to put this, Caro, and I don't want to alarm you but . . ."

"You're going to tell me you've seen Bill Shergold lurking about, aren't you?" the younger woman interrupted, quickly.

"Yes. But I didn't know you knew and I hated the thought of being a scaremonger, especially just now."

"Oh, don't worry. I know, all right. But it only started recently, the prowling at night, that is. Since Chancy left, in fact. I suppose Bill found out about that, although God knows how. He's so damn cunning, that man. That was why I was so doubtful about leaving you alone the day I drove Leo to Bristol. I meant to get back earlier, but we got held up by holiday traffic. I should have allowed for the fact it was a Friday. Was that the reason you looked so pleased to see us?"

"Was it that obvious?"

"Well, I couldn't help wondering. What was Bill up to?"

"Only looking through your kitchen window. Then he must have heard the station wagon and vamoosed."

"Yes, he's a bit of a Houdini. When were the other times you saw him?"

"The day I was coming back late from my trip to the sea. It was getting dark, so I couldn't be quite sure, but I thought someone was looking in through a window at the Daye House. But Jason certainly saw him when he went out to do some night photography. It couldn't possibly have been anyone else. What do you think he actually wants?"

Caroline turned her head away and took a sip of brandy. "It could be that he just wants to intimidate us, or . . . "

"Or what?"

This time Caroline stared her straight in the face. "Look, Jessica. I could be way out, just a silly hysterical woman but, you see, I've always known that Bill Shergold is a bit of a lecher. I never liked the way he looked at me. That was one of the reasons I wasn't sorry to see the dairy go. With Chancy around, I've always felt more secure. It's odd that Bill started turning up in the evenings so soon after he left."

"Does Leo know about all this?"

"He doesn't know the latest developments.

102

But he was well aware of Bill's over-familiarity when he was here. I think he was just as glad to be shot of him as I was."

"Caro, I think you should go to the police." Jessica became suddenly authoritative, the older woman giving advice.

"The *police*!" Caroline's eyes opened wide. "I couldn't do that."

"Why not? You're being harassed. You could get an injunction or something. Stop this man from coming anywhere near the place."

"Then Leo would have to know. And it might antagonise Bill Shergold further."

"Better than going on as you are."

Jessica poured them both some more brandy. Then, even more emboldened, she said, "Since we seem to be having more than just an ordinary conversation, I couldn't help wondering what were the other problems affecting Leo, which you mentioned the other day. Don't tell me if you'd rather not, only this situation does seem to me to need going into seriously. I appreciate your trying to shield Leo but, well, he *is* your husband."

Caroline was silent for so long that Jessica wondered whether she had overstepped the mark, until she heard her reply, "Leo isn't my husband. We're not married. He has a wife, as well as a son of about Jason's age. His wife won't divorce him. He's had to provide maintenance all this time. Of course, they've been living apart for longer than five years. You know, you can get a divorce after two years' separation if both parties agree, and after five if only one wants it. But Leo was very much the guilty party, so to speak, even though I believe Margery was always hell to live with. By the time Leo might have tried to start proceedings, he was in no fit state to do so. That suited her fine. She just hangs on and on. Like a Rottweiler," Caroline added, with an uncharacteristic show of bitterness.

"I see," Jessica said, barely audibly. It was all so much worse than she had imagined. "Have you and Margery ever met?"

"Once. In London. It wasn't very pleasant."

"And the son? What about him?"

There came over Caroline's face that

resigned, hopeless expression which Jessica had noticed before when the girl was unusually distressed. "Leo has wanted to see him. But Margery's poisoned the boy's mind against us both." Then, somewhat defensively, she went on, "Leo and I fell in love when he was a highly successful stockbroker and I was working for some caterers who did directors' lunches for his firm. He didn't take up farming solely because he felt it was something he wanted to do. Our affair caused a much publicised scandal. Margery was vindictive and trumpeted the story all over London. It seemed best for us to . . . well, disappear altogether. Lie low. Now, Leo feels he's been a complete failure."

"And you?"

"Me?" Caroline took another sip of brandy. "I was mad about him at the time. I probably led him on. I'm just as much to blame for the mess we're in. My family has disowned me. I can't run out now. Not on a sick man. Besides, I still love him."

11

FROM where she was gathering some late green tomatoes in the garden in order to make chutney, Jessica did not hear the sound of a motorbike arriving at King's Folly. Behind her, half a mile away, Leo was using a loud whining chain-saw cutting up logs for the winter, a freak gale having brought down an old apple tree. Since his last visit to the specialist in Bristol, he had seemed brighter and apparently found 'wooding', as he called it, satisfying and therapeutic.

She was therefore startled when she suddenly became aware of a young man in leather gear and crash helmet walking towards her down the path from the house. No visitors were expected and it seemed hardly likely that a stray one had arrived without a booking, certainly not so early in the morning.

As the stranger drew nearer, he removed his helmet to reveal a thin, sharp-featured face, framed by long dark hair hanging about his shoulders. She took an instant dislike to him and his greeting, if such it could be called, did nothing to dispel this reaction.

"Hi, there, Missus! Is the old man about?"

She frowned. Presumably he was referring to the owner of King's Folly and thought she was his wife.

"Mr King, you mean?" she replied, stiffly.

"Sure."

The whine of the chain-saw momentarily ceased. She now felt she knew, without a shadow of doubt, who this uncouth young man was but, if her assumption was correct, she was determined to prevent him meeting his father without due warning. It would be better, she thought, for Caroline to handle the situation, much as she longed to protect both her and Leo. But Caroline, unfortunately, had not yet returned from delivering produce to Carsons and had explained that she might be away longer than usual, as she wanted to do some extra shopping on the way back.

"I'm afraid Mr King is busy," Jessica said, playing for time. "Perhaps you could call back later."

His eyes narrowed. "Look, Missus," he went on, in his insolent manner, "I've come a long way. Only a few hours' sleep last night. I need to see your . . . employer urgently. It's important."

As once her anger had risen against Leo, now Jessica found herself defending him at all costs. Although she had never been a person to stand on ceremony, she was also furious with this young man for assuming she was some kind of hired hand. She realised, of course, that she had no proof of his identity and wished she had found out more about Leo's son during her recent heart-to-heart with Caroline. It dismayed her that she did not even know his Christian name, but this was rectified by his next remark.

Almost smirking now, he said, "I'm Pete, the old boy's son. Or long lost son, I suppose you could say. Though I don't imagine he'll exactly want to kill the fatted calf on seeing me. I dare say he'll be gobsmacked. I'm rather older than when we last met."

The whine of the chain-saw started up again and she was afraid Pete might put two and two together and walk on down towards the corner where the noise was coming from. He was evidently determined to accomplish whatever it was he had come to say or do.

Against her will but slightly more graciously, she said, "Perhaps you would care to have a cup of coffee while you are waiting."

"Great," he answered, revealing a younger, less aggressive self.

She led the way back to the Daye House and set about boiling a kettle, spooning Nescafé into a mug, getting out milk from the minute refrigerator and finding some sugar and biscuits, while he looked around with interest.

"These are your . . . quarters?" he asked, obviously puzzled.

"Yes. I happen to be a guest."

"Guest?"

"Yes. The Kings provide accommodation for holidaymakers and very good it is, too."

He stared at her, uncomprehendingly.

"But I thought you were *working* in their garden."

"I enjoy it," she replied, somewhat stiffly again.

He took the mug she proffered and she realised that he thought her mad. The sound of the station wagon returning mercifully precluded any further conversation along these lines.

"That will be Caroline," she remarked, and was mortified to hear him reply, "Ah, yes, the mistress. A bit of a dish, I expect. They usually are."

Anger once again took complete hold of her. How could Caroline possibly cope with this unexpected twist in the saga, a saga which seemed to run the whole gamut of human emotions: guilt, greed, bitterness, sexual desire, weakness, frustration and despair.

From the window, she saw Caroline jump out of the station wagon and start to unload the empty containers. Then she found that Pete had come to stand close beside her and was watching the scene intently. Under his breath, she heard him say, "Strewth! More than a dish."

Glaring at him, she walked towards the

door. "Wait here," was all she said as she went out, closing it behind her.

Once inside the farmhouse kitchen, she told Caroline what had happened as gently as possible, naturally omitting the more lewd of Pete King's observations. To her distress, she noticed the girl go quite white. Then she sat down suddenly and remained silent for several minutes.

"He'll have to see his father, I suppose," she said, at length. "But, oh my God, *why* did he have to come now, just when Leo seems as if he might be turning the corner."

"Does Pete know about his illness?" Jessica asked.

"Hard to say. Margery's probably told him something, but she's a devil for distorting the truth so that she can put Leo in as bad a light as possible."

"What do you think he's come for now?"

"I've no idea. At least, sorry, I suppose I have. It'll be money. Money has always been what Margery wants. Now Pete's left school, for which Leo has been paying, I expect he wants an allowance. I don't think he has a job. Maybe

111

Margery's got fed up with him, as well as Leo."

It transpired that most of Caroline's suppositions were correct. The meeting between father and son, at the instigation of the former, took place half an hour later in the Daye House, while the two women waited in the King's Folly kitchen. It was brief and obviously bitter. Pete King emerged shouting abuse and disappeared in a cloud of dust on his motorbike. Leo also disappeared, back to his wooding.

Jessica, anxious to know what had taken place, did not hear until later that evening when Caroline came across to see her.

"It was as I feared," she informed her. "Margery told the boy she could no longer afford to keep him and that he should contact his father. When Leo tried to explain that *he* had no money to give him either, Pete called him a liar. This will set Leo back more than I dare to think."

Suddenly, she put her head in her hands and burst into uncontrollable tears.

12

THE inhabitants of King's Folly received both good and bad news shortly after Pete's visit. The good news was that Chancy telephoned to say he would soon be coming back; the bad news was the reason. His sister, Kate — unmarried and, as he had once informed Jessica, an altogether more successful artist than he himself — had died.

Jessica, to her mortification, found her initial reaction was one of relief, albeit quickly followed by guilt. But there was no denying the fact that, with Chancy around again, she would be able to make a firm date for leaving King's Folly. The sensible side of her knew only too well that she had become far too involved, that Marianne and Terence and Jason were right to try to discourage her from staying longer, especially as the people with whom she had become so unaccountably friendly had, until that summer, been complete strangers. Yet she knew that she would continue to think about them, would want to keep in touch, know how they fared and would hope and pray that somehow things would improve for them.

She had become increasingly concerned about Caroline, doing her best to get her to visit their GP, Dr Pinnegar, on her own account. She did not like the way Caroline jumped so easily, talked too fast and appeared to have lost a considerable amount of weight which she could ill afford to do. Jessica knew, of course, that it was Leo who was the stumbling block and unless his own mental health improved, there was not much chance of Caroline's doing likewise. Sadly, as she worked through many a sultry late September day, she was obliged to admit to herself that, as Caroline had predicted, his son's visit had sent him a long way back on the precarious road to recovery.

He had ceased any further attempt at 'wooding', and had taken to going for long walks by himself, often not returning until quite late. This worried both women considerably. After Mercedes had gone home, they had started sharing a meal together in the farmhouse kitchen, Jessica having insisted that she no longer wished to be waited on. Leo's own meal was kept warm for him but, more often than not he did not seem to want it and went straight upstairs to bed. The nights were colder now and the dovecot not a suitable place in which to sleep.

On these occasions, Jessica found all her initial indignation and anger with Leo reasserting itself, but it was also tinged with a nebulous anxiety: anxiety about his mental state, his wanderings, their effect on Caroline and the possibility of further complications of an unspecified kind. She was well aware of the tenseness in Caroline which she tried to hide, as they waited for him to return from his peregrinations.

One Thursday evening when Chancy was expected 'probably some time in the night', as he put it, Caroline had at last made the visit to Dr Pinnegar, which Jessica had been urging her to do. His surgery had apparently been crowded and she did not arrive back until around nine p.m. Leo was still out and Jessica, having eaten her own meal, went to take Caroline's out of the oven, only to be told she did not want it. "I'll wait," she said, abruptly, with none of her usual courtesy. "You go back to the Daye. If Leo isn't here soon, I'll come across and let you know."

Miserably, Jessica did as she was asked, her ears straining for the sound of Leo's footsteps or Chancy's car. It would seem that, so far, Caroline's visit to her GP had made her even more on edge. At eleven, true to her promise, she came to tell Jessica that she had informed the police of Leo's disappearance. She said she thought she would go out and start searching for him, but Jessica managed to restrain her, pointing out that it would be impossible in the dark and that, besides, the police would want to question her. Together, they sat silently in the kitchen while Gracie, sensing something was wrong, laid her head on Caroline's knee.

When, shortly afterwards, two police officers arrived, she could only tell them what she had already said on the telephone, that her husband — as

116

she called Leo — was an invalid, suffering from depression, who found long walks therapeutic, but that he had never stayed out as late before.

"And you have no idea, madam, where he might have gone?" The older man, kind and concerned, questioned her gently. "Might he, perhaps, have called in on someone?"

"Oh, no. I'm sure he wouldn't have done that." Caroline seemed quite shocked at the idea. "He . . . has not been very sociable since his illness. In fact, neither of us has."

The interrogation continued in the same courteous manner.

"Did he have any favourite routes, madam?"

"Not that I know of." She paused. "He was fond of wildlife. He had occasionally shown interest in what was being done down at the old gravel pits and the idea of turning it into a nature reserve. But most of the time I think . . . he just walked anywhere. He believed it helped him to sleep."

"You will, of course, let us know at once if your husband returns, madam, but . . . should he not do so, we shall start making an extensive search as soon as it is light."

"Thank you." Caroline's voice was little more than a whisper now.

Still deferentially, the police officer said, "There is just one other point which I should like to ask you, madam. Has anything happened recently which might have caused your husband extra stress?"

An agonised look came over Caroline's face now. Barely audibly, she replied. "I . . . suppose you could say family problems," and left it at that.

"Thank you, madam." He did not probe further.

Family problems, Jessica realised, could have meant anything; but after both men had gone, she could not help wondering whether they imagined that Caroline was the guilty party in some kind of love triangle. Even in her distress, she still looked beautiful, as well as pathetically vulnerable. Jessica felt certain that her questioner had been aware of this. Was it possible that he already knew something about the unconventional set-up at King's

Folly? About Chancy? About the Kings' financial situation? Or were both men starting out on a voyage of discovery, as she herself had done a little while ago?

There was no requesting Jessica to go back to the Daye now. Caroline made some tea and they both sat drinking it, saying little, other than banalities. Rain lashed at the windows and Caroline remarked that autumn seemed to have arrived early. Then, about two a.m., Gracie lifted her head and pricked her ears. Above the storm the sound of a car could be heard. Jessica watched Caroline clench and unclench her hands. Could it possibly be bringing Leo back? Within a few minutes, Chancy was standing in the doorway.

He looked from one woman to the other in bewilderment. "Surely," he began, "I don't deserve a reception committee, especially at this time of night?" Then he stopped suddenly, as he took in the seriousness on both their faces.

"What's happened?" he asked, abruptly.

"Leo," Caroline answered, "is missing."

"Missing? Since when?"

"Since early this evening. He went out walking and hasn't come back."

Chancy sat down. Jessica made a fresh pot of tea and, unlike his customary good manners, he accepted the cup she offered in complete silence.

After a moment, he said, more as a statement than a question, "You've informed the police?"

"Yes. If Leo doesn't return, they'll start searching at daybreak."

In spite of the fact that he had just flown the Atlantic, driven down from Heathrow and must have been extremely tired, Chancy took charge. He insisted that Caroline should go and lie down. He tried to make Jessica do likewise, but she managed to desist. It was, she felt, the only opportunity she might have to talk to Chancy alone about all the developments which had taken place during his absence. She told him about Bill Shergold, about Pete King's visit, the subsequent deterioration in his father's health, Caroline's reaction to this and, with certain reservations, her own fears concerning Leo's disappearance.

Chancy listened carefully, making few

interjections. At the end, to her chagrin, she realised that she had not expressed one word of sympathy about his sister. When she tried to make amends for her omission, he said, shortly," It was best. Her injuries were appalling. Kate would never have been able to paint again, and painting was her life."

13

MERCEDES arrived at six thirty the next morning, almost hysterical. She had been met by a veritable posse of policemen, who seemed to be combing the whole of Folly Bottom and she had been questioned as to where she was going.

"What 'as 'appened?" she asked, as she burst through the kitchen door. There was a wild look in her eyes; her whole being exuded fear.

On being told that Mr King was missing, she became even more distraught. "Poor Meester. Poor Meester King." Then, her expression of grief was somewhat negated by adding, almost in the same breath, "I not like. I not like pleece. I go back to Portugal quick."

Certainly, that day the police seemed to be everywhere. Caroline and Jessica were questioned again, as well as Chancy. "What time had he left Heathrow? Had he passed anyone walking in the area as he neared King's Folly?"

To her horror, Jessica realised that suspicion might well be falling on him. There was an almost copybook example of the eternal triangle: beautiful young wife, sick husband, attractive handyman who lived in a caravan. It was surely inevitable that conclusions would be drawn.

Then, a short while later, a different man from the CID in Bristol called and asked to see Jessica alone in the Daye House.

"You are a guest here, Mrs Milroy, I understand."

"Well, I was, originally. But not now, exactly. I have been helping out while Chancy . . . that is, Mr Lennox has been in America." She thought how odd his real name sounded, never having used it before.

"How long have you been here?"

"About two and a half months."

"Did you know anything about the family problems, to which I understand Mrs King referred last night, other than, of course, Mr King's depressive illness?"

"Yes. I think she was referring to a

visit his son made here a little while ago. He and his father were . . . estranged."

Dear God, she thought, this man's going to ask me about the marital set-up but, mercifully, he continued, "You mean they had a row?"

"Yes."

"What over?"

"Money, I believe." Then, hoping to stave off any reference to Leo and Caro not being married, she went on quickly, "Mr King's son was not the only person who seemed to have some kind of grudge against him. There is a man called Bill Shergold, his ex-dairyman, who was made redundant. He doesn't seem able to forget or forgive. In fact . . ."

"Yes, Mrs Milroy?" He took her up quickly, as she paused.

"He sometimes hangs around here," she answered, somewhat lamely.

"Thank you," he replied, "but I know about him. To get back to Mr King's son. Do you know where he is or where he went?"

"I haven't any idea."

"He was riding a motorbike, I believe."

"Yes." How, she thought, did this man

know so much? And, if so, why bother her except for corroboration. Presumably, the police had ways and means of miraculously gathering information unknown to her. She decided to be bolder. "May I ask, Officer, if you have any theories as to what has happened to Mr King?"

"You may ask, madam, and the answer is, 'Not yet'. At this stage we are keeping an open mind. The state of Mr King's mental health is something which has seriously to be taken into account."

"You think he is dead?"

"The longer he is missing makes that possibility more likely. We have divers down at the gravel pits already."

"*Divers at the gravel pits?*"

"Yes, madam. It would seem a sensible measure. Mrs King mentioned Mr King's love of wildlife." At least, Jessica thought, he keeps conferring on Caroline the status of wife.

When he had gone, she lay down on her bed. She felt more than merely exhausted. The situation had become unreal. She recalled how Bill Shergold had tried to turn her against King's Folly, how she had imagined she would only stay for one night, how she had at first become fascinated and then completely hooked.

An hour or so later, she woke with a start, wondering where she was and what was the time. The dream she had been having was still with her: she had been trying to get to London, but at every turn she took there was a policeman blocking her way. She swung her legs off the bed and stood up. I'm as bad as Mercedes, she said to herself, as she made a strong cup of tea: *I not like. I not like this at all.*

She began to worry about what she had said, or hadn't said, to the CID man. She had been pleased that, throughout the interview, he had referred to Caroline as Mrs King, but now she wondered whether, with his uncanny and lightning facility for amassing information, he was merely being courteous.

This brought her thoughts back to Chancy and her initial fears that he was a suspect, a man who wanted Leo out of the way because he wanted Caroline. He called to see her a little later on. She had been amazed to find it was only just after one p.m. So much had happened. He brought her some sandwiches — hastily cut, with none of Caroline's expert presentation — and a bottle of duty-free whisky, bought at Heathrow.

"I intended this as a present for you," he said. "Naturally, I hadn't thought it would come in handy in quite this way. But I reckoned right now you and I could do with just a little extra fortifying. Mercedes has been too distraught to work, especially after the police tried to question her, so Caro sent her home. She's set on getting back to Portugal as soon as possible and as it's pretty obvious she can't be of any further help in proceedings, I dare say she'll go. Caro herself has gone down to the gravel pits. I tried to dissuade her, but she was adamant. God knows if the police are on the right track. Unfortunately the media's got hold of all this. There was something on the local radio at midday. I suppose it could be on the national news tonight."

"Oh, *no!*" She thought of Marianne and Terence and Jason. Once they knew, they would insist she returned. But she couldn't. She was in it now, up to her neck, as the cliché went.

As she feared, they *had* heard and Marianne rang later that evening, greatly concerned. "Look, Ma, would you like me to come down? It's rotten for you having to go through all this." To her credit, she expressed no word of recrimination, her sole wish appearing simply to be of help.

If Chancy hadn't returned, Jessica felt she might have accepted her offer, but instead she said, "Thank you, my dear. It's very kind of you. But we're all right at the moment. I'll keep you informed."

"But Ma, we hate to think of you mixed up in all this. You don't have to stay, do you?"

This time Jessica's reply was rather more terse. "Yes, I must stay for the time being."

Then, with a distinctly unsettled Gracie at her heels, she went out into the garden to see about the watering. The light was fading and a harvest moon had begun to rise. For some unknown reason, she suddenly thought of the Mertons, the American couple who had been so intrigued at the thought that, long ago, an English king might have been holed up at King's Folly. What on earth would they think about the place now and the sad circumstances which had come upon its occupants so many centuries later. She pictured Frank and Milly back in their home in Idaho. They had given her their address. Perhaps she would send them a card at Christmas. But, on second thoughts, perhaps not. She could hardly put on a Christmas card news which she was increasingly beginning to think would be bad.

As she adjusted the hose and sprinklers, she became a little calmer. There was nothing like keeping busy at a time like this. She supposed that Caroline was still down at the gravel pits and possibly Chancy had gone there also. There was a strange stillness about the place, rather like the one which she had noted when she first arrived.

Long before she heard the sound of a car returning, Gracie lifted her head. Then Jessica realised there was possibly more than one coming along the track. She walked back to the house, trying to prepare herself for whatever and whoever she might encounter.

As she reached the courtyard, she saw three vehicles approaching: a police car, the station wagon driven by the CID man who had interviewed her that morning and Chancy's old rattle-trap, with Caroline sitting in the front seat beside him. As they all drew up, she watched Chancy jump out of his own car and then run round it to help her out. With infinite care, he steadied her as she stood up and then gently shepherded her into the house.

14

THE inquest on the death of Leonard King did not take place for several weeks. So far, all that had been established at the autopsy was that he appeared to have died from drowning. But because of the somewhat unusual circumstances surrounding the discovery of his body in the deepest part of the lake caused by the excavation of gravel near Folly Bottom, countless stories went flying along the rural grapevine: that he had inadvertently fallen over the low parapet of a bridge while under the influence of anti-depressant drugs, that he had purposely committed suicide because of his depression, that he had been pushed from behind by an enemy or enemies out to get him.

The one person whom the police were initially unable to trace for questioning was Leo's son, who would appear to have vanished since his ill-fated visit to King's Folly. Then, about a fortnight after his father's death, Pete was picked up, more or less accidentally, by a roving police car some twenty miles away. He had been sleeping rough, having sold his motorbike and was now living on the proceeds, augmented by one or two odd jobs, such as helping on a local building site and temporarily managing a petrol pump.

When he gave his name and was informed that his father had died, he said, "You must be joking." When further admonished and told that he would be required to report for the inquest, he became truculent; but stronger admonishment left him in no doubt that, if he did not appear on the right date, things would go worse for him. In the event, he did turn up, an unprepossessing character: unkempt, hostile and arrogant.

The courtroom that morning was packed. It seemed to Jessica and Marianne — who this time had absolutely insisted on driving down to King's Folly — that busybodies must have come from far and wide, besides both local and national newsmen. Jessica was distressed to see

Caroline, driven by Chancy, being subjected to a battery of cameras as she got out of his car. She realised it had been a mistake to have allowed him to transport her. It would have been far better if she had come with her and Marianne.

Caroline was the first to be called. She looked pale and drawn as she walked up to the witness box, a slight figure in a black and white check skirt and a black polo-necked sweater, her fair hair drawn back into a neat bun, instead of its usual pony tail. She seemed at least ten years older.

From the very start of the proceedings, Jessica became uncomfortably aware that things were going to be far from easy for her. She took the oath in a dignified manner, but there was a gasp of surprise throughout the court when she gave her name as 'Caroline Frayne'.

"You are not, in fact, the wife of the deceased, Madam?" The coroner, a Dr Wilmot, was a white-faced little man wearing half-moon spectacles, over which he regarded her steadily. He reminded Jessica of a ferret which, considering his job, did not seem inappropriate.

"No."

"But you have called yourself Mrs King for several years, I believe. Why was that?"

So he already knew the situation, thought Jessica. What a lot of detective work must have gone on behind the scenes. She waited, anxiously, for Caroline's reply.

"It seemed the best ... that is, the easiest thing to do under the circumstances."

"Mr King's wife being still alive?"

"Yes."

There was another sound in the courtroom now, a kind of hostile murmur which Dr Wilmot quelled merely by raising a hand.

Out of the corner of her eye, Jessica noticed Pete, slumped at the far end of the bench on which she was sitting. It was impossible to catch the expression on his face, for it was hidden by the long dark hair hanging round it, which she remembered so well from the visit he had paid to King's Folly.

"Mr King had been ill for some time,

I understand," went on Dr Wilmot.

"Yes. He suffered from depression."

"For which he was being treated by his doctors."

"Yes."

Should she not have said "Yes, sir," Jessica wondered, as she listened to Dr Wilmot's next words.

"Miss Frayne, do you know if this depression was inherent in Mr King's personality or were there specific reasons for it?"

"I do not think he ever had it before, but he . . . we . . . lost money farming. It worried him a lot."

"Did he ever give any intimation that he might take his own life?"

She hesitated. "Not . . . exactly."

"But you yourself were afraid of that?"

"It had sometimes occurred to me, yes."

"The night he went missing may have been one of those times?"

"Yes."

"I believe you visited your GP, Dr Pinnegar, earlier that evening, Miss Frayne. Why was that?"

There was a slightly longer hesitation

before Caroline replied, "I hadn't been feeling well. Mrs Milroy thought he might be able to give me something to help me sleep."

"And when you returned to King's Folly around nine p.m. and found Mr King still out, you asked Mrs Milroy to go back to the Dairy, or Daye House, as I understand it's called."

"Yes."

"Then when you went to tell her you had rung the police you also said that you wanted to go looking for Mr King."

"Yes. But she thought it was . . . too dark and wet. That it wouldn't be possible . . . or sensible because the police would want to see me."

Caroline was looking ashen now. Jessica noticed how her hands gripped the rail round the witness box. Dear God, she thought, the girl won't be able to take much more. Whether Dr Wilmot was of the same opinion she did not know but, suddenly, to her great relief, she heard him say, "Thank you, Miss Frayne. That will be all for now." Jessica was sorry he saw fit to add 'for now'.

Chancy was the next one to be called.

He gave oath in a rather impressive manner, his voice calm, collected and extremely clear. He said he had been living in a caravan at King's Folly for four years, that he had gone there originally for a holiday as he wanted to get out of London and was fond of the English countryside. He found that he enjoyed helping the 'Kings' — as he referred to them — and was interested in their various enterprises.

"You did not know before your arrival that they were not, in fact, man and wife?"

"No, sir." Chancy used the last word easily and naturally, without a trace of servility.

"But you discovered their relationship later?"

"Yes, sir. We all three became good friends."

"You were driving back from Heathrow to the West Country on the night Mr King disappeared, I believe. Were you surprised at what you found on your arrival?"

"Yes. I couldn't think what had happened. I walked in and found

Caro . . . Miss Frayne and Mrs Milroy sitting up together in the kitchen at about two a.m."

"And you passed no one walking near King's Folly on your way?"

"No, sir. It was a shocking night, weather-wise."

"Thank you, Mr Lennox."

Pete King was then called. He took his time, sauntering up to the witness box and taking oath in an insolent manner with an odd kind of leer on his face. Jessica noticed that a certain sharpness had crept into Dr Wilmot's voice now. Leo's son was not a young man anyone could possibly take to. He said he had called to see his father some weeks back because he was broke. "But the old man . . . my father," he corrected himself, "seemed to be broke too. Or so he said. Though he and his mistress appeared to be living off the fat of the land, so far as I could see."

Jessica took violent exception to the boy's use of the word mistress. It would seem that the coroner also heartily disliked Pete's disrespectful attitude. "I am not asking you for your opinion of your father's way of life, Mr King." His words, cold and reproving, echoed round the now silent courtroom. "I would like to know what you did after that visit?" he continued.

"I sold my bike. Got the odd bit of work."

"Why did you decide to stay in the neighbourhood, Mr King?"

"Why the heck shouldn't I? It was as good as anywhere. My mother and I don't always see eye to eye. 'S'matter of fact . . ."

"Yes?" Dr Wilmot's eyes, gimlet eyes, stared at the young man.

"Well, as a matter of fact, after I'd had time to calm down, I had half a mind to go and see the old man again, ask him whether I might live in the caravan I saw there. I went back and took a dekko at it once or twice. No one seemed to be living in it. I quite liked it down there. I suppose I might even have put in the odd day's work now and then on the garden at King's Folly like the old lady I saw picking tomatoes. For a bit of ready cash," he added.

Old lady, indeed! It was true, Jessica

supposed, but nevertheless she found herself bridling, as well as feeling shocked to think that Bill Shergold had not been the only one of late who had been prowling around the place.

"And on the night in question when Mr King was missing," she heard Dr Wilmot continue, "were you still in the King's Folly area?"

"No. Same as I told the police. I was doing late shift at Turners' All Night filling station on the Bridgwater Road."

After Pete stepped down from the witness box, Bill Shergold shuffled up and took his place. He was looking larger and more repulsive than ever. His belly seemed to protrude not only over his trousers, but the rail surrounding the box itself. Jessica noticed that his daughter and son-in-law, Edna and Sidney Yates, were leaning forward intently at the back of the court.

In a sonorous West Country burr, Bill stated that his name, somewhat surprisingly, was William Montgomery Shergold. Presumably, thought Jessica, he was a war baby. He said he had been a dairyman when the Kings first took on

King's Folly, but that "they didn't know the fust thing about farmin'."

Once again, Dr Wilmot interrupted to say that he had not asked for the witness's opinions, only direct answers to his questions. "When Mr King," he continued, evidently tactfully deciding to use Leo's name only, "gave up dairying, you were made redundant?"

"Yus. But you see 'e weren't no farmer." Bill Shergold, ignoring Dr Wilmot's reprimand, was almost shouting now. "I kept tellin' 'im the best way to go about things but 'e wouldn't listen. When thic mad cow disease . . . "

Dr Wilmot raised a hand. Peremptorily, he managed to bring the tirade to a halt. "Mr *Shergold*," he said. "I must repeat. I do not want your opinions, merely straightforward answers. I want to know where you were and what you were doing on the night of Mr King's disappearance."

"Me?" the big uncouth man looked affronted. "I were in the Whistling Pig till closin' time, same as my daughter and son-in-law will tell 'ee."

Bill Shergold's daughter did, in fact,

141

nervously corroborate this statement, although Jessica detected a slight hesitation in her husband's voice when he vouchsafed that his father-in-law had his own key and often came in late after he and his wife had gone to bed. On the night in question he himself had been suffering from a heavy cold and so he had gone to sleep in the small spare room and had not actually heard him come home.

Could Bill Shergold, Jessica wondered, have gone elsewhere after his session at the Whistling Pig? She found herself still wondering as she walked up to the witness box. She had never been to an inquest before but, from the morning's revelations, she had deduced that her own part in the proceedings would probably be only minor. She confirmed that she had originally gone to King's Folly for a holiday, but had 'stayed on'.

"Rather like Mr Lennox," Dr Wilmot remarked, though not unkindly.

"Yes, sir." Although she was so much older, she saw no reason why she should not adopt the same attitude to her interrogator as Chancy.

"And you were able to support Miss

Frayne on the night when Mr King did not return?"

"Yes, sir. I hope I was of some help."

"And Mr Lennox, on arrival at King's Folly . . . " here, Dr Wilmot glanced down at his notes, "could not think what had happened when he found you both sitting up so late?"

"That is correct. He was naturally very surprised."

"What took place next?"

"Chancy . . . I mean, Mr Lennox insisted that Miss Frayne should go and lie down. He and I sat up talking."

"What about?"

"I told him certain things which had taken place during his absence in the States. About the visit of Mr King's son and . . . "

"And?" Jessica noticed Dr Wilmot possessed the same quickness and skill as the CID men in getting his witnesses to carry on whenever one of them paused.

"That I had been worried about Mr Shergold seeming to be so often hanging around King's Folly for no apparent reason."

There was a sudden commotion in the

court. Bill Shergold had risen, noisily, to his feet, but was pulled back by his son-in-law.

"Thank you, Mrs Milroy," Dr Wilmot said and, gratefully, she returned to her seat.

He then read out a report from Dr Avery, Leo's specialist in Bristol, which was corroborated by the local GP, Dr Pinnegar. He informed the court that he had been attending Mr King for several years, that his condition varied but that while he had appeared better after his last consultation with Dr Avery, he had gone down badly again after the visit from his son, so that he had recommended increasing the dose of antidepressant drugs pending a further consultation with his specialist. He also stated that Mrs King — as he, like others, referred to her — had naturally been subjected to a great deal of stress and had visited him on the night of the tragedy, leaving his surgery shortly before nine o'clock.

The pathologist then confirmed that Mr King had died from drowning, but owing to the length of time the body had been in the water it had been impossible to estimate the amount of medication taken before death. There was a small cut on the left temple and some bad bruising down that side of the body, caused most likely by it encountering a submerged tree trunk when falling.

Proceedings, Jessica felt, must surely now be coming to an end. It was getting on for one p.m. Then, to her surprise, a smart confident-looking woman was called to the witness box, who gave her name as Miss Monica Arrowby. Puzzled, Jessica felt certain she had seen her before. As soon as Miss Arrowby spoke, she knew exactly where and when. This was the guide at the historic house where she had encountered the Mertons.

Her interrogation did not take long. Monica Arrowby merely stated that she happened to have driven past the gravel pits at about eleven o'clock on the night in question, having been out to dinner. Approaching Folly Bottom, she had noticed the figure of a man standing on a little hump-backed bridge. She remembered thinking it odd because it was pouring with rain. A little further on she had passed a smallish car coming in the opposite direction at high speed. Because of the poor visibility she was unable to see who was driving or whether there was more than one occupant inside. She had hoped that perhaps it was someone coming to pick up the rather desolate character she had seen a little further back. She had thought no more about the incident until she had heard about the tragic events which had taken place on that particular night and had felt she should come forward in case such evidence might be of help.

Dr Wilmot thanked Miss Arrowby and then announced that the court would adjourn until two thirty p.m., when he would sum up. At a local hotel neither Caroline, Marianne, Chancy nor Jessica wanted anything to eat, although the drinks which Chancy insisted on buying revived them a little. They spoke only of trivialities, all minds being on what the coroner would say on their return to the courtroom. Promptly, at two thirty, they were back in their seats.

There was an expectant hush in the place as they heard Dr Wilmot announce, "In the absence of conclusive evidence, I have no other option but to bring in an Open Verdict."

15

THERE was an uneasy feeling of anticlimax at King's Folly following the inquest. Nothing had been established. Several red herrings had been raised, which had only confused the issue.

The one definite and immediate consideration now on the agenda seemed to be the appalling financial situation with which Caroline was faced. King's Folly had been mortgaged up to the hilt. The bank foreclosed. She told Jessica she wished to get away from the place as soon as possible and was almost obsessive about it. "I am fit," she kept insisting, although she looked very far from it. "I can get a cooking job anywhere. I'll go back to London and start again."

This, Jessica felt, would certainly stop further speculation as to a possible relationship between her and Chancy. But the one thing which really laid any further tittle tattle to rest was Chancy's

148

sudden and astonishing announcement that, his sister having been unmarried, he had become the main beneficiary in her will. He had always known that Kate was highly successful, but he had had no idea that she would leave quite such a large estate. He explained that he therefore now found himself in a position to take on King's Folly and, while he would be only too pleased if Caroline were prepared to help him, he quite understood and accepted that the place might hold too many unhappy memories for her.

Under any other circumstances, Jessica felt that this solution, though unconventional, would have been the answer to many a problem. Chancy had hinted that he would not be averse to trying to put into practice Caroline's one-time plan of turning the establishment into a proper country house hotel or maybe some kind of artists' retreat. But even this failed to alter her decision to make a clean break. The possibility that, should she have gone along with either idea, it might have resurrected gossip had, Jessica felt sure, nothing to do with her refusal. Although

Caroline thanked him most sincerely, she said her mind was made up. It seemed that her greatest regret at leaving King's Folly was parting from Gracie. "But it wouldn't be fair," she kept repeating, "to take her to London. She'll be far better off staying here with Chancy."

It soon transpired that Caroline had already gone some way towards organising her future. "I've a splendid girlfriend called Penelope Benson who's married to a barrister," she told Jessica. "They live in Chelsea and she's prepared to let me have the basement of their house pro tem. They've got two kids and she's suggested I might like to become a kind of general factotum in her household until I've sorted myself out."

The only favour that Caroline appeared willing to accept from Jessica, however, was a lift in her car when the time came. Therefore, on a cold blustery late October day, the two of them set off, the emotional side of the leave-taking mercifully kept well under control, the journey itself conducted mostly in silence. Although negotiations with the bank for Chancy to become the new owner of the property were far from settled, he himself was 'prepared to hibernate', as he put it, throughout the winter. "I'll keep the garden ticking over and think of you two safe and warm in the big city, far from the wilds of Wessex. Please, both of you, keep in touch."

When Jessica dropped Caroline at the Bensons' house in Chelsea, she echoed Chancy's words about keeping in touch. But despite Caroline now thanking *her* most sincerely for all the help and support she had given her over this 'ghastly summer', there was something deadpan in her expression, as if she were forcing herself to draw a veil over all that had happened. Somehow, as Jessica drove away, having thought it best to refuse Penelope Benson's kind offer of tea, she had a feeling that it would be she herself who would have to make the first move towards any meeting. Caroline had certainly changed. She was a very different person from the lovely outgoing young woman who had cooked dinner for her on that first never-to-be-forgotten night when she had arrived at King's Folly. All that had taken place since, had made Caroline old beyond her years.

The flat, when Jessica entered it, seemed oddly impersonal. It was clean and warm and her caretaker cum cleaner had obviously diligently polished her antiques and done all the shopping she had requested by letter. But she knew it was going to be difficult to pick up the threads again of what had been, even at best, a rather mundane existence. She recalled how someone had once said to her, after they had both read the same book, "I liked it. It rang true. I know these sort of things do happen, but not, I'm afraid, to me."

Jessica had to admit to herself that something *had* happened to her now: something so curious, so totally unexpected, that six months ago she would never have thought it possible. Besides keeping her from planning any future moves for herself, it had made the very thought of them seem singularly dull. She would have to do *something*, but imagining herself behind a desk doing a voluntary job at, say, a citizens' advice bureau or some charitable organisation filled her, somewhat to her mortification, with downright distaste. The real life drama that had brought her out of herself was something which, however fraught and tragic, made it now almost impossible to settle down again.

She was certainly pleased when Marianne asked her to spend a weekend with them when she knew Jason was coming home and, on her return, she forced herself to telephone a few friends in London. But it was Caroline who was constantly in her mind and, one evening when she felt she had left it long enough, she rang the Bensons. A child's voice answered her call and immediately went away to seek, as she hoped, Caroline. But it was Penelope Benson who picked up the receiver. Her voice sounded harassed and weary.

"I'm sorry, Mrs Milroy, but Caro's gone to the doctor."

"Doctor? She's not ill, is she?"

Again there was a slight wariness as Penelope replied, "No. Not really. Just a check-up. Would you care to leave a message?"

"Well, yes. I thought she might like to come to dinner sometime."

There was obvious uneasiness in Penelope's manner now. "It's very kind of you, Mrs Milroy. Perhaps Caro could give you a ring. I believe she has your number." There came the sound of a child screaming in the background and the conversation was hastily cut short.

Jessica went back to her sitting-room, concerned and puzzled. Caroline had certainly shown great signs of stress since Leo's sudden relapse and, naturally, more so after his death. But Jessica had hoped that the 'clean break', which she had so courageously set her heart on might have worked wonders. She wished now that she had rung earlier, instead of holding back for fear that she might prove too unwelcome a reminder of a period in Caroline's life which she was trying so hard to forget.

It was several days before she telephoned. Jessica had almost given up hoping that she would. Her voice sounded even more wary than Penelope's. She apologised for not having done so earlier, but explained that she had been rather busy with the children, who had not been well. Jessica felt that somehow this was merely an excuse. Nevertheless, she repeated her invitation to dinner, saying, tentatively, "Perhaps one day next week?" This, she thought, would give Caroline time to back out or think up some other excuse.

"Why, yes." All at once, the voice altered and became brighter.

"How about Monday or Tuesday?"

"I'll come Monday, if I may." The acceptance sounded genuine, as if in the space of a few moments Caroline had completely changed her mind.

But her appearance the following Monday evening gave Jessica a shock. Getting away from King's Folly had certainly not had the effect for which she had hoped. There was a haunted haggard look about Caroline, worse than Jessica had ever witnessed. Surely becoming general factotum in the household of such a pleasant person as Penelope Benson could not have made her this exhausted.

Suddenly, a thought so horrible, so terrible came into Jessica's mind that, even as she helped Caroline off with her coat, she found herself trembling. Could it, was it, remotely possible that Caroline knew more about Leo's death than she had ever admitted?

Then, taking a firm grip on herself, Jessica led her into the sitting-room and managed to say, "What would you like to drink? There's some white wine in the fridge or would you prefer something stronger?" The girl certainly looked as if she could do with it.

"Neither, thanks."

"Oh, but surely . . ."

"No," Caroline repeated, abruptly. Then she sat down and faced Jessica across the small sitting-room. Her next two words sounded as cold and bleak as Dr Wilmot's 'Open Verdict' at the inquest.

"I'm pregnant," was all she said.

16

THERE was silence after Caroline's startling announcement. Then Jessica went across and put her arms round the girl, who managed to whisper, "Thank you."

Trying desperately to think of the best way to handle the situation, Jessica was infinitely relieved when Caroline spoke again. "It's Leo's, of course. I'm sure you realised there had never been anything between Chancy and me."

"Yes, my dear."

"Leo was so much better, you see, after the last time I took him to Bristol to see the specialist. But it was a total surprise when he . . . well, when he seemed to want to sleep with me again. He . . . we . . . had been so long without. I wasn't prepared. Neither of us were, I suppose."

"Yes, I see."

"I wasn't going to let the opportunity slip. It was like a miracle. Such a relief."

"Yes, I'm sure. I understand."

"I knew you would. I wanted to tell you. In fact, I was going to tell you after I got back from the doctor's that night, the night Leo was missing. Then it was all . . . so awful."

"Leo never knew?"

"Oh, no. At least, sometimes now I wondered if he guessed, whether it wasn't only Pete's appearance which set him back again, made him feel such a failure, made him take his life, that is, if he did. Do *you* think he did, Jessica?"

"Caro, I don't know what to think."

All she could think of at the moment was how terrible it had been of her ever to have doubted Caroline. How could she have let a shred of suspicion enter her mind. Especially after hearing all the evidence at the inquest. Thank God for Monica Arrowby, who had seen what must have been Leo's figure by the gravel pits at eleven p.m. Thank God Caro had got back to King's Folly at nine. Thank God that she herself had managed to dissuade her from going out again looking for him. Thank God it had been confirmed that Chancy never left Heathrow until midnight and the post-mortem had established that Leo's body had been in the water some time before he arrived home.

Gently, Jessica said, "What are you thinking of doing now, my dear?"

Caroline blew her nose. "I would never ever entertain the idea of an abortion. I've always wanted a child. Leo knew that. I was afraid I'd missed the bus. Penny has been wonderful. She's dying to go back to work. She's an art editor. She and her husband want me to stay on, look after their children, and my own baby, when the time comes."

On the face of it, it seemed to Jessica the best possible solution in the troubled circumstances. But of the long term situation, she hardly dared to think.

The dinner, which she had taken such pains to prepare, remained spoiling in the oven. Neither Jessica nor Caroline wanted any. The latter explained that one of the reasons she had been so doubtful about accepting Jessica's invitation was because she suffered from evening — as opposed to the conventional morning — sickness. "Apparently, pregnancy does take some people this way. I'm told it will soon pass."

Before she left, she managed to eat a small amount of what Jessica felt to be merely a burnt offering. Then, as she got up to go, Jessica asked, "By the way, have you told Chancy?"

Caroline shook her head. "But I will. I'll write tomorrow. I felt I should like you to know first."

Never, thought Jessica, as she went down in the lift with her and pressed some cash into her hand for a taxi before Caroline had time to desist, had she come across anyone who had had such a raw deal. The trauma of her own disastrous marriage and divorce seemed negligible in comparison.

She was not surprised when Chancy telephoned her at the weekend.

"How is she, Jessica? I've heard the news."

"Putting on a brave face, as you might expect. Thank God for these Bensons."

There was a pause, before he continued, "Of course no one else knows down here, except, presumably, Dr Pinnegar, who examined her the night Leo went missing.

I'm thankful professional etiquette between doctor and patient prevented it coming up at the inquest. I'm afraid it may add fuel to the further enquiries when it does come out."

"What do you mean? Further enquiries?"

"Well, it seems someone wasn't at all satisfied with the coroner's verdict. The police have been to see me twice. I gather there's a lot of undercover work going on. I think you may be questioned again. They've got your address, of course, and I was obliged to give them Caro's London one."

"Do you really think they'll bother either of us again? I mean, it was so plain that . . . we were together that night and can't help any more."

"Oh, I know. Your guess is as good as mine. But I suppose an Open Verdict is what it implies, always open to question."

After they said goodnight, Jessica went over the inquest once more in her mind, as she had done countless times since it took place. Somehow, in spite of them both being unattractive and undesirable characters, it was difficult to think that either Bill Shergold or Pete King would have gone so far as to harm Leo, other than by verbal abuse and harassment. It would, of course, have been better to have had more conclusive evidence and she was curious about the person who was anxious to obtain it.

She did not have long to wait. The woman's voice on the telephone next day was authoritative and aggressive — no one she knew. And yet, quite suddenly, she did.

"Mrs Milroy?"

"Speaking."

"I want to come and see you."

There was no 'I would like to come and see you', or 'I wonder if I might come and see you.' 'The caller made it quite clear she was coming, willy nilly.'

"May I ask what you want to see me about?"

"You may. I believe you knew my late husband. I'm Margery King. Will you be in this evening?"

Jessica was hardly ever discourteous, nor did she lie, but Leo's wife's manner incensed her. "This evening is not convenient," she replied, coldly. "If you could tell me what it is you want to know, perhaps it could be done on the telephone."

"I hardly think a man's untimely death is a subject to be discussed on the telephone. Tomorrow morning, shall we say, about ten thirty?"

"Tomorrow evening," Jessica found herself replying. "I shall be free at five."

Other than that she was obviously an embittered woman, Jessica had always found it hard to picture Leo's wife. Vaguely, she had imagined her blonde, smart and around fifty. She was therefore surprised to be confronted by a small dark woman with heavily mascaraed eyes and wearing a long black mackintosh cape. There was something witchlike about her. She seemed well past middle age, older than Leo had been, in fact. Her jet black hair must surely be dyed. However, now that Margery King had arrived in person, Jessica felt she could do none other than offer her a cup of tea or coffee.

"No thanks." The refusal was swift, sharp and to the point.

Once she had removed her cape and had sat down in exactly the same seat as Caroline had occupied a little while ago, the contrast between the two women was so marked that Jessica could quite understand what had prompted Leo to change from one to the other — although she supposed that Margery, in her younger days, could have been more attractive, before the lines of hardness in her face had developed, before the abrupt unsociable manner had taken hold.

"You stayed at King's Folly this summer for quite a time, I believe, Mrs Milroy?" she began.

"Yes."

"How did you find my husband?"

"Sometimes he seemed better than others. He was certainly suffering from depression."

"Who wouldn't be, with what he had to put up with?"

"I'm sorry. I don't quite understand . . ."

"You know perfectly well what I'm driving at. Miss Frayne can lead any man a dance."

Jessica said, quietly, "I am a friend of Caroline. She did her very best to look after Mr King and their establishment. She worked incredibly hard all the time."

"I'm not saying she didn't. She is

evidently a woman with enormous energy. She was working quite hard when she first seduced my husband and then went on to make his life hell as she exercised her undoubted sexual magnetism on another paramour."

Jessica stood up. "Mrs King, I am not prepared to continue this conversation. I have the greatest respect and admiration for Caroline Frayne. I do not know why you have insisted on coming here unless it is merely to vilify her."

"I have come as Leo's wife." The resemblance to a witch became suddenly more marked, as Margery King fixed Jessica with her black boot-button eyes. "I have never been happy about the Open Verdict. Not happy at all. I intend to do everything in my power to discover the truth. I shall leave no stone unturned. You must know as well as I do that Leo was murdered."

17

AND she wouldn't stop, Jessica knew, after Margery had left. She would go on and on. She would go and see Caro next.

Quickly, Jessica went to the telephone. Fortunately, Penelope Benson answered it, explaining that Caro was out with the children. She listened carefully to what Jessica had to say and assured her that she would do her best, both to warn Caroline and prevent the 'wretched woman' from coming anywhere near her.

Then she surprised Jessica by suddenly asking, "You don't happen to know whether Leo had a life insurance policy, do you?"

"No. But why do you ask?"

"It's just that . . . well, some time ago Richard was involved in a case which hung on whether a man had committed suicide or been murdered. If he was murdered his wife could claim insurance, but with suicide it's rather more tricky, especially if the policy has been recently taken out. Of course, that wouldn't apply in Leo's case and, besides, I dare say it's all different nowadays, particularly with an Open Verdict."

"Oh," was all Jessica could reply. I should have known about this, she thought. I'm so ignorant of so many things. But if there *is* anything in what Penelope says, it could well have a bearing on Margery's eagerness to find out the truth. If Leo had had life insurance and been murdered, presumably she would stand to benefit, still being his wife. Although he could easily have let it lapse owing to his financial difficulties. Or had he struggled to keep it up because of some edict imposed by Margery's solicitors? What a strain that must have been on his dwindling resources, if so.

"I suppose Caroline could simply refuse to see Mrs King," Jessica now said, but without conviction.

"Yes. Although it might look worse, mightn't it? Fortunately the pregnancy doesn't show yet. She lost such a lot of weight at the beginning."

"But seeing Margery would be awfully

distressing for her."

Penelope, ever resourceful, suddenly hit on an idea. "I know what. I could send Caro and the children to my mother for a bit. She lives in Sussex. It might stall Madame King."

Jessica became confused. Margery King, having harboured such bitter resentment against Caroline for so long would continue to do so. She would bide her time and when that time did arrive, it might be obvious that Caroline was carrying a child. What Margery was after, probably quite apart from the question of life insurance, was proof that Caroline and Chancy had been conducting an affair and wanted Leo out of the way. She was such an incredibly vindictive woman and the revelation about Caroline's condition would be exactly the ammunition she was looking for.

"By all means ask your husband about the situation when he comes home," Jessica said, slowly. "But it might be better not to do anything about sending Caro to Sussex just yet."

They rang off. The conversation had

been, like the inquest, worrying and inconclusive. Jessica felt as if she were treading on quicksand. Perhaps it would be a good thing to get out and go for a real walk on terra firma. She had always found physical exercise or work therapeutic. Putting on a headscarf and padded jacket — except on occasions, she had always dressed as a countrywoman in London — she set off across Hyde Park.

They were into November now. It was cold and raw. Fallen wet leaves dappled the paths. There was a definite air of *fin de siècle* about her little sojourn. She knew that Marianne and Terence were delighted she was back in town and that the King's Folly affair was really none of her business; yet her mind couldn't leave it alone. She still felt as much involved as if she had known the chief protagonists all her life.

Would the situation be any better by Christmas? She doubted it. Marianne had asked her to join them, as usual; but she could raise no enthusiasm this year. Why, whatever happened *vis à vis* Caroline and Margery King, the former would still be suffering. She would be further along the way to joining that sadly-named group in society: a one-parent family.

The walk calmed her a little, as Jessica had known it would. But she still felt tired, more tired than she could ever remember. Far from helping her, she realised that her attempt at a holiday, while certainly jolting her out of herself, had certainly not been the kind of break that she had had in mind. It had developed into a kind of nightmare, one which was still going on.

The telephone was ringing when she got back to the flat. To her surprise, it was Simon, her son, calling from Paris. Since his remarriage, followed by such a peripatetic life, she and he seemed to have drifted further and further apart. She knew that Helen, his new wife, was, to a large extent, instrumental in this. She did not want him to have anything to do with his former one or his son or, indeed, his mother. Jessica felt that emotional insecurity had much to do with Helen's determination to make him sever, completely, any links with his past. Left to himself, Jessica liked to believe that Simon, for all his profligate ways, would have kept in touch, at least with Jason. But Helen, the only daughter of rich parents, saw to it that any such inclination was carefully deflected by dragging him round the world, so that they were seldom in England.

"Hi, Ma," he began, in his usual nonchalant manner. "Long time no see."

The fact that, had he really wanted to, he could have got in touch before, was invariably and tactfully overlooked. She herself, knowing the situation between man and wife, had long ago given up making the first move. She had no wish to make things more difficult for him, but it distressed her that he did not occasionally manage a quick call, just to see how she was getting on. When he did telephone, though always glad to hear from him, she was uncomfortably aware that there was usually some ulterior motive. It was as if, rather like his father, moral or familial responsibility seldom occurred to him.

She was therefore slightly mollified when he announced, "I've been trying to get you for some time."

Doing her best not to wonder if this could really be true, she replied, "I've been away, Simon."

"Yes, I know. I rang Marianne in the end."

Again, cynically, two thoughts came into her head: Helen must have been out whenever he had called and that he evidently had something important to say.

"I gather you've given up working for old Frobisher and decided to go down to the West Country for a holiday."

"Yes."

"Pretty traumatic one, by all accounts."

"Well, it wasn't quite what I expected."

"Too bad. You really ought to plan a bit more, Ma. Go somewhere where you're taken care of and you don't have to think. Like Helen, for instance."

"Helen?"

"Yes, well, she's been feeling a bit run down so she's gone to South Africa to stay with her parents."

"Oh, how nice." She wondered why he hadn't gone too.

"I didn't go," he volunteered, as if

in answer to her unspoken question, "because I've got one or two projects on the tapis."

Again, she wondered what they were. So far as she could recall, Simon always spoke of having 'projects on the tapis', or 'irons in the fire', money-making enterprises which never seemed to make any money.

"So while Helen's away, I thought I might pop over to London, see how you're getting on and tie up a few ends."

"I see." Did she see? Too much? The fact that Helen had let him off the hook was, in many ways, a bad omen. For such a possessive woman to go off to her parents and leave her husband free to contact his former wife, let alone his mother or some other female, must mean, surely, that something was wrong. Please God, there wouldn't be a second divorce.

"I wondered if you could put me up, Ma, just for a night or two."

Jessica had known it was coming, as soon as he had said something about London.

"Well, yes," she replied, slowly. "Have you a date in mind?"

"I thought about this Friday," he answered, quickly, "if that's OK with you."

18

FRIDAY seemed very far from 'OK' when the day actually dawned. For one thing, Jessica woke up with a bad cold; for another, Chancy telephoned later that morning to say that apparently Margery King was staying at Chandlers Hotel. He had been given this information when he had called in at Turners' Garage and found Pete King working there full time. Having had a watertight alibi on the night of Leo's death, the boy said that both he and his mother were anxious 'to get to the bottom of things' and he seemed to be relishing the business of further investigations. Mrs King had just rung Chancy and was coming to see him on Saturday afternoon.

"I'm very sorry," was all Jessica could say, wondering why the woman had not yet contacted Caroline, for presumably she would by now have obtained her London address.

"I'm not bothered," Chancy replied. "I just want to get it over with."

"You'll let me know how the visit goes, won't you?"

"Of course. In a way, Jessica, I, too, rather welcome what's going on. I think the whole district feels the same. Rumours and counter-rumours have been flying round since the inquest. The police seem especially interested now in that other car the Arrowby woman passed. So far, there's only been one response to their appeal for any driver who was in the vicinity that night to come forward. He happened to be the local rector!"

"Does Bill Shergold ever bother you these days?"

"No. But I understand his daughter is ill. A nervous breakdown from all the strain."

After their conversation ended, Jessica looked at her watch. She would like to have rung Simon to suggest he stayed at a hotel, but realised that he must already be on his way. Under any other circumstances, she would have welcomed a chance of seeing her son without his wife, but what with Chancy's news and her own indisposition, she felt she could have done without any guests. Mercifully, she had finished her shopping the previous day, as well as preparing her small spare room which still bore, unmistakably, the signs of having been occupied by Jason in his younger years.

She was rather shocked on seeing how much his father had aged when Simon arrived at five that evening. He was very pale and there was a flabbiness about him that she had never noticed before. He did not look like a man happy to have any 'irons in the fire' or anything 'on the tapis'. She offered him tea but he said, if she didn't mind, a drink would be 'more to the mark'. His tendency to cliché-ridden conversation seemed to have increased. It did not take her long to discover that, as she had feared, he had come to London to talk to his solicitor about getting a divorce.

As gently as she could, she asked him if Helen had left him, distinctly remembering, as she did so, the countless other women in his father's life.

"There are faults on both sides," he answered, quickly and defensively.

177

Jessica wondered if he considered Helen's possessiveness to be one of hers, this business of never allowing her husband the freedom which William had simply taken as some male right. Jessica recalled him saying, "After all, I do provide for you, Jess. You have a pretty good lifestyle. I can't see why, if you don't want to sleep with me any more, you can't turn a blind eye on my little peccadilloes." After a constant stream of them, she had finally snapped. She realised that Helen had snapped somewhat sooner and presumed that Simon's adultery was the real cause of the break up; although considering how his wife kept him on such a tight rein, it was amazing how he had managed to get away with any extra-marital liaisons at all.

It occurred to her that as this was Friday, Simon would be unable to see his solicitor until Monday, at the earliest. What would he do? What should *she* do? They were poles apart for spending the weekend in such close proximity. I must *try*, she kept telling herself; but her concern over Caroline, both Simon's and Chancy's news, plus her worsening cold — which her son appeared not to notice — made her feel totally wretched.

"I nearly put you off," she said, at one point during the evening, when he was on his third whisky and she was on her one and only.

"Oh?" He looked surprised.

"Well, I've got this cold. I don't want to pass it on."

"Don't worry about that. I seldom catch them. A pity your holiday didn't set you up for the winter, Ma. What exactly happened?"

It was the first direct question about herself that he had asked her, yet she did not feel able to reply properly, nor that he was particularly interested. It would take too long. It was all so improbable. She simply answered, "The man who owned the place where I stayed died."

"Died?"

"Well, either he committed suicide or it was an accident or he was killed. An Open Verdict was brought in at the inquest. Enquiries are still going on."

"Really? As I said on the telephone, you ought to take more care where you jazz off to, Ma. I'm glad you're back in London. Jolly nice for me, too," he added, "seeing that we don't get a chance to see all that much of each other."

Far from worrying about how he would amuse himself over the weekend, another more agitating thought came to her. How long was he intending to stay? Now that his rich wife had departed, was he short of cash?"

Quickly, she changed the subject. "Will you be going up to Oxford to see Jason?"

He became evasive. "I'm not sure. I'll have to think about it. I'd rather like to get things sorted out with my solicitor. I'd prefer to present the boy with a *fait accompli*. I mean, it'll be my second time around, so to speak."

She wondered how her grandson would take it. One never really knew what went on in children's minds, but perhaps it had been as well that he had been so young at the time of the first divorce. Sometimes, she couldn't help feeling pleased to think she might have been a help to Jason during those early years, that she hadn't done too bad a job at providing the extra security he needed.

180

And perhaps, now that he was out in the world, a second divorce wouldn't have too much of an impact. After all, it wasn't as if he had ever seen much of his father. Although Simon was her own flesh and blood, she was glad that his son seemed to have taken so completely after his mother. She could not have asked for a better daughter-in-law nor, for that matter, a son-in-law — as she thought of Terence — even though they were not really connected in any way.

After she had given Simon dinner and gone to bed early, excusing herself on account of her cold, she found she was quite unable to sleep. She had never been given to self pity, but it was difficult not to regret that, at a time of life when she might have been able to sit back and take things easily, problems kept piling up. Terence and Marianne had been so right in wanting to get her out of King's Folly. If only she hadn't opted for a summer holiday so soon after her job with Gerald Frobisher packed up, she might well have now been on some winter cruise, not available to cope with anyone else's troubles, particularly those of an unpredictable son.

After a bad night, she was thankful when he announced the next morning that he had thought better about seeing Jason and that he might 'trickle up to Oxford' after all. But her relief was quickly dashed when he added, 'later next week'. When, that Sunday, Chancy telephoned to say he thought he would like to come up to town the following weekend, if it was convenient, and tell her about Margery's visit, she felt emboldened to ask Simon just how long he was thinking of staying.

He seemed astonished. "Well, Ma, I'm fancy free and footloose, as they say. Naturally, I don't want to be an imposition, but I felt you wouldn't mind my occupying your spare room for a while unless, of course, you have another guest coming."

"As a matter of fact, I have. I want to put him up next Friday. Someone I met in the West Country."

"*Aha!*" Simon became slightly arch. "Was *that* why you stayed so long at this . . . holiday camp?"

Fury mounted within her. "Simon,"

she said, "I am coming up seventy. The person to whom I am referring is at least twenty-five years younger. He has taken on King's Folly which is not, by any stretch of the imagination, a holiday camp."

"OK, OK, I take your point. But Ma, I'm in a bit of a spot. I'll clear out of here next weekend but could you, by any chance, lend me a thou? Just till I get straightened out. Things aren't easy, as you can imagine, at the moment."

Ruefully, she agreed to write him a cheque once she had rung her bank. She knew it would never be repaid. Suddenly, she recalled how, just before she had left for the West Country, she had, somewhat morbidly, gone through her will and had imagined that when she died, Simon would come rushing back from wherever he was, intent on giving her a champagne send-off. Well, at least that wasn't likely now, thank goodness. But it saddened her to feel that her only son had made so little of his life, that he was on the downward slope. She wondered where he would live, how he would manage. He had

had a good education but he had never applied himself to anything, had given up on a variety of jobs. Was his only hope now to find another rich wife? It would not be easy. Once upon a time he had been very good-looking. He still had charm, when he cared to exercise it, but his pallid face and his paunch gave him away. There was something degenerate about him.

He became more and more moody as the week went by, going out but not saying where and when indoors he lapsed into long silences, a drink invariably to hand. She sensed that he was aggrieved she was not willing to accommodate him longer and as she wished him goodbye she felt, both physically and metaphorically, they had come to the parting of the ways.

19

AS she had anticipated, Jessica found Chancy's visit very much more pleasurable than her son's. The difference was quite remarkable. He was the perfect guest, arriving with two bottles of excellent sherry and laden with produce from the King's Folly garden. "I'm still reaping the rewards of all Caro's hard work and foresight," he explained, as he hauled a large black dustbin liner into her kitchen, crammed with carrots, parsnips, potatoes and winter greens.

Moreover, he seemed to want to take Jessica out to restaurants all the time and had to be restrained. "You can't," she insisted. "You must allow me to serve the meals I've actually prepared." But she was obliged to give way on Saturday and agreed to let him give her and Caroline lunch at a quiet place he knew of in Chelsea.

Jessica was glad to find her looking better and Caroline herself was delighted

185

to see them both, eager for any news Chancy was able to supply. It was only to be expected that one of her first questions was "How is Gracie?"

"Gracie's fine," he replied. "I know she's being well looked after. I've left her with Mercedes's son, José, and, believe it or not, Mercedes herself. Apparently his wife, Muriel, has run off with some ne'er-do-well so Mercedes felt it her duty to return to England, despite the winter, and take care of him and her beloved granddaughter."

Chancy had already told Jessica a great deal about what was going on at King's Folly but now, encouraged by Caroline's interest, he enlarged on the situation, putting forward, as delicately as possible, a few theories of his own. He said he felt there must be a 'wild card' in the whole affair, that someone wasn't coming clean.

"I'm still in the dark, of course," he said, "like everyone else. It's just a hunch of mine."

"Do you think Bill Shergold really did go straight home after his session at the Whistling Pig that night?" Jessica asked.

"Well, his son-in-law doesn't seem to have known, but his daughter said he did, didn't she? Besides, it wasn't much of a night for prowling around, even though Bill's obsessive grievance was certainly getting the better of him. That, coupled with his intake of alcohol, might have caused him to do anything."

"How ill is the daughter now? You said something about a nervous breakdown," Caroline broke in, obviously sympathetic towards anyone with mental trouble.

"I'm afraid she's had to be taken off to some NHS institution near Bristol. I believe Sid, her husband, goes to see her every evening."

"How are he and his father-in-law managing?"

"I should think Sidney Yates is pretty good about the house, although he's got a full time job at Carsons. But one mustn't forget, of course, that Edna was a working wife at the Tourist Board in the summer months and went off early on the bus each morning. So for all I know, Bill can cook the odd sausage, that is, when he isn't too sozzled."

"How long do you think Margery King

is intending to stay at Chandlers?"

"Your guess is as good as mine. I think she found me a most disappointing interviewee. I suppose she's hoping to pin the blame on you or me or both of us but, failing that, anyone to prove that Leo was murdered."

"Why do you think Margery never called to see Caroline after she came to see me?" Jessica took over the questioning this time.

"I think, to put it bluntly, she just wants to collect as much ammunition as she can before she does that."

"Is what she's doing legal?"

"God knows. I suppose there's nothing to stop her. And Leo was, officially, her husband."

Jessica noticed Caroline put up a hand to her face. She suddenly looked tired. Jessica asked whether she would like to come back to her flat for the rest of the afternoon, but was not surprised when she refused. "Penny and Richard are going out tonight and I've promised to look after the children," she told them.

Just before Chancy took his leave next day, Jessica asked him something which she felt she should have done earlier. There had been so much discussion about the other issue that she realised she had omitted to enquire how he himself liked his new role as owner of King's Folly.

"I like it more and more," he replied. "I didn't say too much in front of Caro, but I really am keen on turning the place into something special, better than Chandlers. I want it to become somewhere where people come year after year, hopefully to paint. A friend I know, Peter Blakeley, has offered to advise me. As a matter of fact," and here he stopped and seemed slightly embarrassed, "well, I told Ma King this and she was obviously put out. You know, it was plain that I had no intention of marrying."

So that, Jessica thought, after he had gone, means that Margery will now be hell bent on attacking Caro alone. But how, exactly? Perhaps the truth will never come to light. She remembered a forensic pathologist once telling her at some dinner party that murder was seldom black and white. "There are things which no one knows about. Areas of grey," he had said and she wished he wouldn't go on. She did not care for the subject, wasn't interested. It had never entered her head that she, personally, could ever be affected by it. How wrong I was, she thought, as she sat down and picked up the Sunday papers. What a lot I am learning in my old age.

The paragraph at the bottom of one page was so small that she could easily have missed it. Yet it seemed to leap out at her, drawing her eyes towards it like some magnet. *West Country Mystery,* she read. *Investigations are still going on following the inquest into the death of Mr Leonard King, 56, a landowner who was found drowned last September near his home, King's Folly. Mr King had been suffering from depression for some time. His widow has left the area and the estate has been bought by an American, Mr Charles Lennox.*

So much for press accuracy, Jessica thought. Caroline was not Leo's widow, King's Folly was not an estate and Chancy was not an American. If reporters couldn't get their facts right, perhaps it wasn't any wonder that no one else seemed able to either.

Presently, with an effort, she glanced cursorily at the rest of the papers, but even the headlines failed to interest her. She closed her eyes. Pictures of King's Folly kept coming into her mind: the night she arrived, Caroline bringing her dinner, Gracie bounding back across the field after taking Mercedes home, her first encounter with Leo in the dovecot, the arrival of his son, the night she saw Bill Shergold lurking about when she was all alone and then the other terrible night when Leo was missing.

The ringing of the telephone broke into her reverie. It was Jason, calling from Oxford.

"Is Dad still with you? Mum says she thought he might be."

She was astonished. "He left Friday, Jason. I thought he was coming up to see you."

"Well, he hasn't turned up. But then, you know Dad. How did you find him?"

She realised that neither Jason nor Marianne would have known anything about another possible divorce. But it wasn't for her to enlighten them, was it?

Simon had been singularly cagey about the matter since seeing his solicitor.

"I thought," she answered, truthfully, "he seemed a bit down."

"But presumably he's been let off the hook for once?" Again she wondered how she should answer. "Helen's gone to visit her parents in South Africa," was all she replied.

"I *see*," Jason said, in a way which made her aware, as if she wasn't already, that her grandson was no fool.

20

CHRISTMAS loomed. Jessica shopped, but without enthusiasm. She received a brief, even curt, note from Simon saying he was back in France, staying with a friend. She imagined this would almost certainly be a female one. He made no mention of failing to see Jason, nor of repaying the thousand pounds — not that she expected he would. Nor did he refer to any future plans. There was no address on the top of the letter and she feared that the breach between them had widened to such an extent that it could never be healed. Remorse overcame her. He was her only son and somehow she had failed him.

Caroline came to see her quite frequently and she marvelled at how much easier she found it to show compassion to someone who had only come into her life a short time ago. Somehow their mutual heartache only seemed to strengthen the rapport between them. For the moment, she decided to give up all ideas of getting herself any work, voluntary or otherwise.

The last time Chancy telephoned he said he thought Margery King was still in the district, but he wasn't sure. Jessica tried to prepare herself for what she felt certain would soon be the inevitable confrontation between Leo's wife and Caroline.

But what she was not prepared for was, on coming back from Oxford Street one afternoon, finding Margery sitting in the hall of the block of flats where she lived, obviously waiting for her. The caretaker had told her that Mrs Milroy was out, but had been unable to refuse her admission to the building itself.

Tired and caught off her guard, Jessica asked Margery to come back later, but was defeated by the wretched woman following her to the lift and more or less forcing her way into it alongside her. Once inside the flat, almost before Jessica had had time to put down her parcels, she said, "I saw your protégé this morning."

"Protégé?"

"Yes. A most devious young woman, who also seems to be in a most interesting condition."

"Miss Frayne is not my protégé, nor is she devious."

"No? Well, you two are very much in cahoots, aren't you? Why did she ask you to return to that outhouse or dairy or wherever you were living on the night Leo was missing? There must have been a good two hours when you and she were apart. Plenty of time for her to go out again."

Jessica stared at her. Then she said, quietly, "I should have heard a car if Caroline had left King's Folly."

"Perhaps she went on foot."

"*Mrs King*, don't be so *ridiculous*."

"The gravel pits are well within walking distance."

"You can't possibly be suggesting . . . "

"I am at liberty to suggest anything I like. I did a lot of homework before returning from the West Country. The police were most interested. I must say I'm surprised that the question of those two hours before Miss Frayne reported my husband missing has not come up before, especially at the inquest. I happened to be there. At the back. Perhaps you didn't know?"

"No. I didn't know."

"Naturally, you were too taken up with being a star witness."

Faced with the woman's hostile insinuations, Jessica simply went to the door and held it open.

"Well, you can't deny I have a point," Margery King said, as she followed her, slowly. Her eagle eyes, coupled with an unpleasant sneer did not make a pretty picture. "Of course, there is another alternative," she went on, as she made her exit. "Perhaps you yourself went out. Apparently the car which Miss Arrowby passed was not a large one. My son, who is now working at Turners' Garage, tells me your own is not exactly a Rolls Royce."

After Margery King had gone, Jessica sat down, abruptly. She felt faint and slightly sick. Did Margery imagine that she or Caro or both of them had pushed Leo into the gravel pits? It was all too preposterous. She dreaded to think what had transpired at her meeting with

Caroline. Once or twice she was on the point of telephoning the Bassetts, but held back. Perhaps it might be better to wait until Caroline telephoned her.

It was not until early the following morning that Penelope rang. "Jessica. Caro's in the Charing Cross Hospital. A miscarriage. She's asking for you."

Not trusting herself to drive, Jessica flung herself into a taxi and went straight there. But on arrival she found she need not have hurried. A staff nurse told her that Caroline was under sedation and that it might be best if she came back a few hours later. Was she, by any chance, the girl asked, as Jessica started to walk away, Miss Frayne's mother? The young lady who had brought the patient in seemed unsure about her next-of-kin. Jessica shook her head, suddenly remembering how Caroline had once mentioned that after she had taken up with Leo her family had disowned her.

Miserably, she went down the escalator and out into the Fulham Palace Road. She had had no breakfast but, not feeling like eating anything, she went into a café and ordered a cup of black coffee. Then, anxious and restless, she went out and walked towards Hammersmith Bridge, where the sky and water seemed to match her mood, reflecting each other in a curious metallic light while the cries of seagulls presaged a coming storm. She had never minded London in winter before. The run-up to Christmas had been quite exciting, especially when Jason was small. She recalled taking him to Hamleys or to see Father Christmas at one of the large department stores.

Her thoughts went back to Caroline and how she had said she always wanted a baby. After the sickness and the initial shock of discovering she was pregnant had worn off, she had seemed, in a quiet way, to be looking forward to having one. Some of her innate optimism and energy appeared to have returned; although now, Jessica could not imagine what would happen.

It was cold standing on the bridge and she shivered slightly. A woman with a child in a pushchair struggled past her. She looked poor, agitated and pinched. Jessica could not help noticing that she wore no wedding ring. A sudden thought came into her head which she did her best to stifle. Vindictive and evil as Margery appeared to be, could she, in the long run, have inadvertently saved Caroline from a future which surely, at the very least, would be fraught with difficulty. Slowly, she turned and walked back to the hospital.

This time, on arriving at the ward, a Sister led the way into a small side room, opened the door and said, quietly, "No more than five minutes, please." Jessica went over to where Caroline lay, her left arm attached to a drip, her face drained of all colour and her eyes closed.

"It's Jessica," was all she could say, taking her hand.

"Thank you for coming."

After a moment or two, she continued, barely audibly, "It was a girl. Leo always wanted a girl." Then they said no more until the Sister reappeared and Jessica realised her time was up. "I'll be back tomorrow, Caro," she said, leaning down to kiss her.

"How bad is she?" she asked the Sister when they went back to her office.

"She's lost a lot of blood, but she'll

be all right. There's no husband, I take it?"

"No."

"You knew her well? And the lady who brought her in, of course?"

"Yes. I should like you to have my name and telephone number."

Jessica watched as the Sister made a careful note of both.

"If there is anything she requires, you have only to ring."

"Of course. We will let you know."

Once outside the hospital, Jessica found it was raining, but fortunately a taxi drew up to deposit another visitor and she was able to get straight into it. Huddled in the back, an overwhelming depression took hold of her. The trauma surrounding Leo's death seemed to have gathered momentum. His witch-like wife had stirred the pot all right, bringing the situation nearer to boiling point. Something, as Jason would have said, would surely have to give.

21

WITH all that had happened since the summer, Jessica had forgotten that it was some time since she had had one of her regular check-ups with her doctor. She had been far too preoccupied with other people's troubles to worry about any of her own. Although she had appreciated that Marianne's and Terence's desire to get her away from King's Folly made sense, she had never considered that she was at any real risk.

But after visiting Caroline again the next day, distressed at finding little improvement in her condition and feeling utterly wretched when she returned home, she was not so sure. The raised blood pressure which Dr Sheldon had diagnosed years ago had never really inconvenienced her. She was aware that he liked to monitor it, while relieved that, so far, she had not been obliged to take medication. Now, after a second restless night, during which her heart seemed to be beating unnaturally fast, she decided to ask him for an appointment.

To her astonishment, Dr Sheldon did not take her blood pressure once, but three times, allowing an interval of five minutes between the second and third readings, while she lay resting on the couch in his consulting rooms. Then he looked at her sternly.

"Whatever *have* you been doing with yourself, Jessica?" The way he framed his question left her in no doubt that things were not good.

"I've been away . . . " she faltered.

"On holiday?"

"Yes. Well, no, not actually. It was meant to be but I suppose you'd say I got sidetracked, involved in the problems of the people I stayed with in the West Country."

"So it was no rest cure?"

"No."

"Then I suggest you should now have one. After all, I seem to remember you telling me back in June that you'd given up your job."

He went over to his desk, sat down

and started writing something, while she rolled down her sleeve and put on her coat. "You must take one of these pills night and morning and I'd like to see you again in a week's time. I'd also like to hear you've booked up to get right away, perhaps on some sort of cruise. With a friend," he added, as he handed her a prescription.

Why did he say that, she wondered. Was he concerned at her going alone?

"I'll come back in a week," she said. "But I'm afraid I can't possibly go away again. There's still so much to resolve."

"How do you mean?"

"It would take too long to go into it," she replied, not wishing to tell him that she had planned to look after a young woman who had just had a miscarriage. She also decided to say nothing about Simon. She had never been a person to confide in others. "I just have to be around until things are sorted out," she went on, somewhat lamely.

"Christmas?" he hazarded. "What are you doing then?"

"Marianne and Terence want me to go to them but . . . "

He interrupted her quickly. "No buts. You should go, Jessica. Take a good break. You must, for once, look after yourself."

She kept thinking of his last words as she went home. Obviously, she wasn't going to be any help to anyone if she became ill. She wondered just how high her blood pressure was. She hadn't liked to ask. Besides, she wasn't exactly sure what it should be. She had always tried to ignore it, yet had never quite been able to. Since it was first diagnosed, she had done her best to be organised, ready for any eventuality, just in case. She thought of her will which she sometimes, morbidly, re-read and how she had done so just before setting off for her so-called holiday.

Then she took hold of herself. She would simply carry on as planned and hope for the best. She would go to Marianne and Terence for Christmas and look after Caroline meanwhile, trusting that she would then be well enough to go with the Bassetts to Penelope's mother. She would say nothing to anyone about what Dr Sheldon had said. Keeping silent seemed far and away the best thing to do.

The foreign voice on the telephone a few days later was loud and excited and took her completely by surprise. Where on earth had she heard it before? Then, listening to the repeated "Meeses Milroy, Meeses Milroy," she realised who it was on the other end of the line.

"Why, *Mercedes*! How nice to hear from you. How are you?"

"Me OK, Meeses Milroy, but José not good. I come back from Portugal to look after him and leetle Menina. You remember?"

"Why, yes." She wondered whether or not to say that she knew about José's wife leaving him, but was forestalled having to make any decision by Mercedes continuing, "His wife. Muriel. She run away. Make 'im very sad. Bad lady."

"I'm so sorry, Mercedes." She wondered what was coming next.

"I like to see you. And Meeses King. You come King's Folly for Christmas, yes?"

"Well, no, actually, Mercedes. I am going to my family and ... Mrs

King" — she thought it best to stick to the name Mercedes had always known Caroline by — "she has not been very well, I'm afraid."

"Too bad. I sorry. Perhaps you both come New Year? Is not the same here. Not at all. I cannot go work because have to look after Menina. José work. Rain every day. José very unhappy. Muriel, bad lady," she repeated.

"Will she come back, do you think, Mercedes?"

"Nobody know. José say man came and took her in car. Bad man. I think it best if I take José and Menina back to Portugal. No good here. Not any more."

Poor woman, Jessica thought, as she put down the 'phone. She was obviously pathetically lonely and upset. She did not like the English winter and now she was forced — or had forced herself — to suffer it in order to look after her small granddaughter and cuckolded son. Jessica had only caught sight of his wife once, but she had a vague recollection of a brassy young woman with a lot of blonde frizzy hair. She must have been extraordinarily heartless to go off and leave not only her husband but her two-year-old daughter.

Unsure whether it might bring back too many distressing memories, Jessica did not mention Mercedes's telephone call when Caroline came to stay a little later. She was pale, withdrawn and obviously still weak, although she insisted she was not. "It's all wrong," she kept saying, "descending on you like this," to which Jessica replied, "You didn't descend on me. I wanted you to come. Good as the Bassetts are, their house with those small children wouldn't be the best place for you to recuperate just now. Penny and I agreed that this was the most sensible solution."

But it was very plain that, having been so active and used to taking charge, Caroline found it difficult to allow Jessica to do much for her. Occasionally of an evening, she would open up, going over the events of the last few months. Once she said, "I wish I could think it doesn't really matter what exactly did happen on that awful evening, Jessica. I mean, Leo's dead now and he was very unhappy.

Maybe he would never have pulled out of that depression. I wish his wife could just leave the thing alone. Richard says that even if she was thinking about the insurance money in the beginning, it's probably all right now. I'm sure it's just her awful thirst for revenge driving her on, rather like Bill Shergold's. Such a pity when I think . . . well, I know Leo and I did wrong, but I believe he had to put up with an awful lot before he and I ever met. He was such a nice man. I do wish you'd met him before his illness."

On another occasion, her mind suddenly went off on a different tack, as she said, "Do you think all that happened is retribution for what Leo and I did? Our come-uppance, so to speak?"

"No," replied Jessica. "I know people sometimes feel that way. They say to themselves, 'I'm ill' or 'I'm being punished because I did this, that or the other.' But then think of all the people who lead blameless lives and are stricken down with the most appalling misfortunes. It's often the really bad lots who get away with murder."

She hadn't meant to say the word. It

had slipped out. But later on in bed she regretted how insensitive it seemed under the circumstances. Besides, it was such a stupid expression. People who got away with murder were not likely to spread the news, so how did anyone ever know they had committed it?

And the more she lay awake thinking about how ineptly she had handled the conversation, she knew that she had been definitely dishonest in her somewhat assertive remarks about retribution. Did she really mean what she had said to Caroline? Wasn't she herself full of self-recrimination, deserving of a come-uppance, particularly after Simon's visit? She wondered where she had gone wrong in his upbringing: allowing him to be sent away to boarding-school? Shielding him from any knowledge of his father's peccadilloes so that the boy found William's happy-go-lucky relaxed attitude to life a preferable example to her own? And surely it would have been better not to have kept falsely praising her son's many impractical projects and then making excuses for them when they invariably failed? But perhaps her worst sin of all was the way she seemed to be forever compensating for her own inadequacies by caring for others rather than Simon. Was it really so surprising that he had turned out as he had, when his own mother had turned him out of her own home in favour of someone he might well have thought aptly named: Chancy, a chance acquaintance?

22

IT was only a fleeting idea, so fleeting that Jessica sometimes wondered how she had ever entertained it. Yet, in the days running up to Christmas, it persisted, coming and going in her mind in troubling fashion, popping up when she least expected it, such as when she was buying a new suitcase for Jason or ordering wine to be sent in advance to Terence and Marianne.

The day before Christmas Eve, while she was packing to leave, she decided to telephone Chancy. "I wonder," she said, "if I could possibly come down to King's Folly early in the New Year. There's something I'd like to thrash out with you."

He sounded delighted. "That would be splendid, Jessica. Why not spend the actual New Year with us? You'd be quite comfortable, I think. I've installed a married couple. Believe it or not, I'm giving a small party."

She was doubtful, both about the party — which she knew she would not feel like — and the travelling. "It's very kind of you," she replied, "but I believe I'll come by train when all the festivities are over, I don't fancy a long drive midwinter. Let's say I'll come a few days later, when hopefully British Rail will be back to normal."

Throughout Christmas she did her best to push the matter from her mind, focusing her attention on family matters. She was charmed by her grandson's witty descriptions of university life. He was so obviously enjoying himself, that she was temporarily lifted out of the curious, almost sinister miasma into which she seemed to have got herself. It did not surprise her that the only communication anyone received from Simon was simply a card for Jason, who she was relieved to see simply accepted it with a wry smile. She was also relieved when, possibly thanks to tact on all sides, the question of King's Folly never cropped up until after Jason had departed for a ski-ing holiday and she herself was preparing to leave. Then, suddenly, Marianne said, "Won't you stay longer, Ma? Surely you don't *have* to get back to London, do you?"

Jessica supposed it had to come sooner or later. "Thank you, my dear," she answered, "but I think I must. As a matter of fact, I've promised Chancy I'll go down to King's Folly after the New Year."

"*King's Folly?*"

It was easy to detect not only Marianne's concern but scarcely disguised disapproval. "Must you?" she said, bluntly.

"Well, yes."

There was a short silence before her daughter-in-law continued, "Ma, I know it's no business of mine, but you're not still bothering on with that extraordinary affair, are you?"

She couldn't lie. All she answered was, "Let's say there's still a lot of unfinished business."

"Such as?"

"Leo's death is a mystery which has never been solved."

"And you want to go on being Miss Marple?"

The question was put quite kindly but somehow it hurt, even though Jessica knew that Marianne did not intend it to.

On the way back to London she kept thinking about her last remark. Was that what Marianne really thought of her? Agatha Christie's elderly amateur detective. But perhaps her daughter-in-law was right. She was certainly elderly and she did so badly want to find out the truth, partly to satisfy her own curiosity but chiefly, she liked to think, because of a genuine desire to help Caroline, who she felt would never be able to make any reasonably happy life for herself, unless the uncertainty surrounding Leo's death was cleared up once and for all.

It snowed over New Year. She thanked goodness she had elected to go to the West Country by train. As she set off from Paddington, she wondered what the steep climb up through Folly Bottom would be like; but then she consoled herself with the thought that Chancy, who was meeting her, would sure to be well prepared for all eventualities. He would have a fourwheel drive vehicle plus chains if necessary.

This proved, indeed, to be the case. He

greeted her at Bristol with enthusiasm, carrying her suitcase out to a brand new Range Rover, where she was given a second overwhelmingly enthusiastic welcome from Gracie. Having had a rug placed solicitously over her knees, they set off, Chancy remarking, "After all the festivities, this time of year is always a bit doleful, isn't it? Your coming is a godsend. One gets geared up for Christmas, keeps the adrenalin going for New Year and then, what have you? A long hard slog till the spring."

It was good to find that her presence was so much appreciated by both man and dog. "But Gracie can't possibly remember me," she said, still fending off canine demonstrations of affection from the back seat.

"Of course she can. You'd be surprised. As a matter of fact, there are a lot of people here who remember you well. Of course it goes without saying that Mercedes can't wait to see you. I met her taking her granddaughter for a walk the other day. When I said you'd be coming to King's Folly soon, her face lit up. She's hating being back in England just now.

This snow must be the last straw."

"Is there any news of José's wife?"

"Not a lot, I gather the chap she went off with is the ne'er-do-well son of a man who's some tree planter about twenty miles away. Apparently it's an affair which has been going on since the summer. Mercedes is usually so voluble, but she kept quiet about this because she felt it was such a disgrace. So, of course, did José. Being a staunch Catholic, I don't suppose there's any question of divorce."

"I'll call and see her tomorrow." It did not seem the time to go deeper into the subject she most wanted to talk about.

The climb up to King's Folly was, just as she had anticipated, hazardous. Even the new Range Rover with Chancy's skilful driving, stalled once or twice. "Until we get a better road," he said, once they had reached the top. "King's Folly is still a summer place."

Yet considering how Chancy had once referred to an intention of 'hibernating' throughout that winter, Jessica was astounded at all the improvements and alterations which had been set in motion

216

in the comparatively short time since she had left. The Daye House, in the process of enlargement, was more or less under wraps. The back of the farmhouse itself was also being extended, Chancy told her. But the front, now floodlit in the snow, made her journey, even if it had been taken for so sombre a reason, seem more than worth while. She recalled how she had often wondered what King's Folly would be like in winter. Now she knew.

For someone who had lived for several years in a caravan, Chancy had organised his more permanent accommodation perfectly. The couple he had mentioned, a Mr and Mrs Woolland, seemed excellent, the bedroom she had been given more than comfortable and the dinner that evening almost up to Caro's standard. Afterwards, she found she was tired and was grateful for her host's insistence on an early night and breakfast in bed the following morning.

It was not until eleven a.m., when they were both sitting in a sun-filled drawing-room, that Jessica said, "José's wife, Chancy. Does she drive a car?"

He looked at her, startled. "My God,

Jessica, how should I know? You'd better ask Mercedes. Why?"

"Well, there's never been any satisfactory answer to that second car in the mystery, has there? The da Silvas' cottage is about the nearest to where it all happened. By the time the inquest took place, Mercedes had been allowed to go back to Portugal and José and his wife were never called. I mean, on the face of it, why should they have been, and yet . . . "

Chancy continued to stare at her in astonishment, even with a certain admiration. "What, exactly, are you suggesting?"

"Might it not have been possible for Muriel or, perhaps, her lover, to have been hurrying — Monica Arrowby said the other car was going fast, didn't she? — and . . . well, there could have been some sort of accident."

"An accident at which someone didn't stop?"

"Yes."

Chancy got up and paced about the room. "It's possible, Jessica," he said, gazing out of the window at the bright white landscape. "Obviously the lovers wouldn't want it to come to light. No more would José. But you'll have to go carefully, won't you, asking any questions?"

"Of course," she replied, "very carefully."

23

MERCEDES greeted her that afternoon with, if anything, more fervent demonstrations of pleasure than Chancy or Gracie. She appeared almost out of control, flinging her arms around Jessica and repeating several times: "*Que prazer em ve-la*", whilst ushering her into the small front room and apologising for the toys on the floor, where her granddaughter sat, wide-eyed and thumb in mouth.

"I get you tea or coffee, Meeses Milroy. Or maybe something stronger? A leetle *vinho*, yes?"

"A cup of tea would be lovely, Mercedes, thank you."

The excited woman ran out into the kitchen, while Jessica did her best to entertain Menina by pushing towards her the small present of a woolly horse which she had brought. This only succeeded in eliciting a piercing howl and Mercedes came running back, swept the little girl into her arms and bore her upstairs where the howls, though certainly less piercing, persisted for a good ten minutes.

Meanwhile, Mercedes returned with the tea, pouring out a cup for Jessica and saying, "I sorry. She tired. She stop in a minute. She not used to strangers. No one come here. You first visitor for long time. Thank you for present."

"But I'm so sorry to have upset her."

"No, no. She go to sleep soon. Poor *criança*. Today José give notice at job. We all go back to Portugal next month. Plenty family look after Menina. Father get another job. Him good carpenter."

"Muriel . . . " Jessica began, tentatively.

Mercedes almost spat. "Bad woman. How you say? Good riddance to bad rubbish? Better Menina not see her again."

"You have no news of her mother?"

A curious expression now came over Mercedes's face. If Jessica had not known her she might have thought it was sly, but she realised that the woman was possibly debating with herself how much private information she should vouchsafe to her visitor.

"We have news," she began and then, suddenly, once started, the story of Muriel and her transgressions came out in a veritable torrent of condemnation.

"She living over Hinchcombe way with wicked man. He not work proper. Him gambler."

"What's his name? How did she meet him?" Jessica asked, when she managed to get a word in edgeways.

"Fergus. Fergus Bailey. He come to gravel pits sometimes. See manager about planting trees by new lake. Muriel often take Menina for walk there. Then one day she say she have this job. Evening job so I could look after Menina when I get back from King's Folly. Says she help Manager. She was secretary before she married José. Manager give her work to do and then go home. She stay on in hut all alone. At first I thought maybe she . . . how you say? Unfaithful with Manager. But then, one evening when José came home early, I go gravel pits. Very careful. I look through window. I see Muriel with other man, this Fergus . . . " Mercedes covered her face with her hands. "Terrible. Terrible."

"Did you say anything to her or José?"

"Not that night. Then José find out too. He very upset, but couldn't stop her. She, how you say in England? Hussy? My son, good kind man. Too kind."

"I'm so sorry, Mercedes." Somehow, in the face of the woman's anguish, it hardly seemed right to probe further; yet surely that was what she had come for? And it wasn't as if Muriel or her lover were exactly exemplary characters. Far from it.

While Jessica was hesitating how best to breach the subject, the problem was suddenly solved for her by Mercedes saying, "When Muriel gave up her job she would go down to pits and wait for Fergus to pick her up in car. Then they went further away for . . . " Mercedes covered her face in her hands once again, not being able to give expression to anything approaching fornication.

"Muriel never drove herself, Mercedes?" Jessica broke in quickly.

"No. Well, not then. But she always after José to buy her car. I think she drive now. Fergus teach her."

"How often did she go out with him?"

" 'bout twice a week."

It seemed now or never. "Mercedes," Jessica said, "Can you remember the night Mr King went missing? Was Muriel out with Fergus then?" She felt almost elated, as if she were getting somewhere at last. A Learner Driver. She could have struck Leo, knocked him over the little bridge. It was almost too good to be true. Maddeningly, she watched as Mercedes took her time, thinking and frowning.

Presently, she replied, "I not know. Long time since Meester King die."

"Yes. Over three months. But, Mercedes, I was wondering if you remembered what day of the week it was, whether Muriel was out?"

The poor woman became flustered and Jessica realised she had gone too far. Naturally, Mercedes could not be expected to understand what she was getting at. Why should she? She had been back in Portugal long before the inquest. She would have known nothing about it, wouldn't have understood what it was, most likely. Nor would she have a clue as to what an Open Verdict meant. As for all the dissatisfaction afterwards and the investigations carried out by Margery King, all that would have been a complete mystery. To her, Caroline was still the late Mr King's wife. José would scarcely have enlightened her. He was a quiet reserved man and would probably have reckoned his family had enough trouble as it was.

Suddenly, Mercedes brightened. With almost childlike pleasure, she smiled and clapped her hands together. "I tell you one thing, Meeses Milroy. Muriel never go out on a Thursday." Far from resenting being interrogated, the woman now seemed delighted to have been able to supply an answer.

This time, it was Jessica who frowned. Thursday was the night when Leo had gone missing and died.

"Are you sure, Mercedes? I expect, perhaps, *sometimes* Muriel went out on that evening."

"Oh no, Meeses Milroy. *Never.*" Mercedes was quite certain, emphatic even. "Fergus never came for her on a Thursday. That was the night he always went to the dogs."

Jessica hardly knew whether to laugh

or cry. The situation had taken such an unexpected twist. She felt totally exhausted and frustrated. With relief, she caught sight of the Range Rover stopping at the gate. "Ah, there's Mr Lennox come to collect me. I must be going," she said, and stood up.

"You'll come again though, Meeses Milroy? Please?"

"Yes, I'll try, Mercedes. I'm not quite sure how long I'll be staying. Give my regards to José and thank you very much for the tea."

I've been a fool, she said to herself as she walked down the garden path. A silly meddling old fool. I'm as bad as Margery King. I've handled it all hopelessly. I've upset a dear simple unsuspecting foreigner. I got a bee in my bonnet. Why couldn't I have left the thing alone, as Terence and Marianne wanted me to? It's as if there's some kind of jinx on King's Folly. It's a folly all right. Though Chancy seems to be making out.

"Any luck?" he enquired, as he helped her into the front seat.

"No," Jessica answered. "How wrong

can one be. It seems that Fergus and his car would have been nowhere in the vicinity the night of Leo's death."

"How did you discover that?"

"Mercedes said that he always went to the dogs on Thursday!"

He smiled at her. "In more ways than one, I dare say," he remarked, drily.

She was silent. Then he went on, "Jessica, you mustn't take it to heart so much. Besides, supposing Mercedes *had* said the lovers were out driving near the gravel pits that night. I don't quite know how you would have set about informing the police. I mean, there was no proof. It was just a hunch. But a good one," he added, quickly.

"Thank you," she answered. "I'm obviously no Miss Marple. I'll try to forget all about it, except . . . "

"Except what?"

"Well, I know Caro can't. It would have been good to get to the bottom of it all for her sake."

24

BACK in London, throughout a cold bleak January, Jessica did her best to settle down and reorganise her life. Thankfully, she received no more visits from Margery King, but Caroline often came to see her of an evening when the Bassett children were in bed and their parents not going out. It seemed as if she, too, was making a valiant effort to forget King's Folly, to make a new start and let bygones be bygones. Yet Jessica felt that probably both of them were still putting up a front, albeit a commendable one. Having told Caroline of her abortive and ridiculous — as she now thought of it — visit to King's Folly, they avoided the subject. Nevertheless, Jessica was sure it was always in the back of their minds.

Although her doctor had been pleased to find Jessica better on the whole, he once again suggested that she could do with another holiday — "a more satisfactory one, this time", he had joked — and it occurred to her that she might ask Caroline to accompany her on some kind of cruise. She reckoned she could just about afford a short one for the two of them and it would certainly comply with her GP's idea of not going alone. Yet something told her that it wouldn't work. In their separate ways they both seemed to be marking time, concerned with unfinished business.

As a temporary measure, to fill her days, Jessica pulled out some of the sketches she had done at King's Folly with the thought of reworking them, but she soon abandoned the idea. For one thing, they reminded her of what she was trying to forget; for another, she realised that they were hopelessly mediocre. She wished she could play bridge like so many of her contemporaries, but felt that she had left it too late to learn. One day she called in at the local citizens' advice bureau thinking she might be able to help there, but it seemed that her age and lack of qualifications were against her.

Often, Jessica longed for her old job back: the regular contact, the simple yet meticulous work she knew she could do, the kind which gave structure, even discipline, to her days. She recalled how engrossed she used to become, listing and cataloguing the various purchases which Gerald Frobisher made, how carefully she would handle them, appreciating the smooth feeling of leather, the smell of old parchment. But nowadays she sometimes seemed beset by a nebulous fear, a claustrophobic feeling that greyness was enveloping her. No longer useful, as she once had been, to Jason and Marianne, or Gerald Frobisher or Caroline, she lacked a *raison d'être*, other than the elusive and frustrating hope of seeing an end to the question mark over Leo's death.

Marianne, coming to London on the excuse of visiting the sales, sensed the despair in the older woman but seemed powerless to help. Any suggestion that Jessica might come and stay with her and Terence temporarily or even permanently, was met with gratitude but firm resistance. "I'm looking forward to the better weather," Jessica would reply. "This is always a bad time of year. It will be so much better when the daffodils are out in Hyde Park."

Reporting back to Terence, Marianne said, "If only she had more family. She's only got us. Simon's such a dead loss. In fact, he might well be dead for all she hears from him. And what with her job folding and Jason growing up and probably feeling her age she let the King's Folly affair take over and get completely out of proportion. As far as I can gather, she went there at New Year genuinely thinking she had all the answers and when she realised she hadn't, she felt she'd made a fool of herself."

Marianne's summing up of the situation was well-judged. Throughout an equally cold February, Jessica's spirits were at a low ebb, temporarily raised by seeing how much better Caroline had begun to look. She was far less pale and tense and sometimes she even laughed, especially when she brought Penelope's children to tea. Such afternoons certainly left Jessica in a slightly happier frame of mind.

At the beginning of March, she was scanning, as usual, the names in the obituary columns of *The Daily Telegraph*, when one near the beginning caught her eye. *Arrowby* was an uncommon name and she wondered if it could be a relative of the Monica Arrowby she had seen only twice in her life, but who had provided such unexpected and significant evidence at Leo's inquest. Jessica had invariably imagined her a spinster, probably living with an elderly parent, or parents, a rather pathetic figure trapped by duty and a need to earn a living, venting her dissatisfaction with her lot by a half aggressive, half defensive manner.

Putting on some glasses, Jessica began reading, with mounting disbelief, *ARROWBY. — On March 4, MONICA JANE, suddenly, beloved only daughter of Mary and the late Reverend Guy Arrowby of Long Buckley* . . .

Jessica sat quite still and read the notice again. There was no doubt about it. She knew that Long Buckley was a village not far from the stately home round which, during the summer months, Monica had spent her days conducting rubber-necks such as herself and Milly and Frank Merton. She wondered what *suddenly* signified. Would she ever know? It was such a blanket term: Heart failure? Accident? Operation? But whatever the cause of Monica Arrowby's death one, or perhaps two, things were certain: the only person who had been anywhere near providing a clue to Leo's death was now dead herself; and she, Jessica, had at least been right about the unmarried only daughter/parent relationship.

Although the news had surprised her, she did not feel it was of any real consequence so far as clearing up the mystery of Leo's death. It was not as if anyone considered that Monica would ever have been able to throw any more light on the situation. She had said her piece at the inquest, firmly and concisely. There had been a car, fairly small and going fast, she had stated, which she had passed after seeing a lone stationary man standing by the low parapet on the bridge by the gravel pits, and she had hoped that the driver was going to pick up this solitary figure who seemed to be waiting for someone.

Nevertheless, sometimes in odd moments, Jessica could not help thinking that there was now less hope than ever of finding out what had happened in the area on that fateful night getting on for six months ago. The passage of time, the unexpected sudden end to another life — that of a middle-aged woman who had actually *seen* Leo just before he had drowned — depressed her even further. It was as if, bit by bit, pieces of the jigsaw were becoming lost irretrievably, leaving behind an unsatisfactory picture for those who desperately wanted it completed. For although the police were still keeping the case open on their files, she suspected they were losing interest. Even Margery King appeared to have ceased her activities or, at least, had ceased to bother her or Caroline.

Then, one day when the long-awaited spring arrived and Hyde Park was splashed with islands of yellow daffodils so that at last Jessica's spirits lifted a little, she received a letter from Chancy which lifted them further. He did not often write, preferring to telephone fairly regularly, and she was intrigued to find quite a long missive after opening the envelope. The sun was shining and she took it out with her to read in the small private gardens below her flat. "I thought it best," he began,

to put all this down on paper, because I'm sure you'll want to have a good think about it. Apparently the place where Monica Arrowby worked is being taken over by the National Trust. As you probably recall, it has a very valuable library, which she was in the process of re-cataloguing and bringing completely up-to-date when she died. Naturally, that put paid to that, but the authorities are anxious to get the job finished. Remembering you used to work for an antique book dealer, I wondered whether you'd have any interest in taking it on. I gather there's about two or three month's careful listing left to do. It goes without saying that they want someone completely trustworthy and knowledgeable. I couldn't help thinking of you. All expenses would be paid regarding your accommodation and travel. Remuneration to be negotiated. *You could stay at King's Folly — nice for me!!* if you wouldn't mind the daily journey.

Anyway, this is to give you a rough idea. Colonel Tranter of Long Buckley is the one-time agent and the man to contact. I've got to know him quite well and he seems a pleasant competent sort of chap. He has an invalid wife and I suspect that is why he took early retirement last year, but he has agreed to come back and help in an advisory capacity to see to the hand-over. I remembered you once told me your man was called Frobisher and when I mentioned this to Tranter he said there would be no need for any further reference. Apparently Gerald Frobisher was the best in his field.

I gather Monica's mother went to pieces after her daughter died and has been whisked off to some residential home nearby. Monica's death was pretty horrendous. Her car skidded round a bend and went down a grass slope. She wasn't found for hours.

To turn to a happier subject: it really is lovely here just now and plans are under way for a better road to King's Folly . . .

Jessica closed her eyes and lifted her face to the sun. The warmth, though imperceptible, seemed a hopeful sign. She was being offered a job, a job she was sure she could do and a paid one at that. She knew the area and the people in it, especially Chancy. She would be able to work at her own speed, unsupervised. If only for a few months, she would have a *raison d'être* again. It was all very well for her GP to go on about a holiday, but she was not a holiday person. Never had been. She would have to tell Marianne and Terence, of course; but it wasn't as if she would still be concerned with King's Folly. She would be doing something different, something for which she was eminently qualified and which, hopefully, might restore her self-confidence.

25

COLONEL THOMAS TRANTER, as Chancy had said, proved to be an extremely competent man of about fifty. He was good-looking, courteous but somehow strangely remote. Had it not been for his invalid wife, he seemed far too young to have ever thought of retiring. She sensed that he had no time for small talk and this was something she appreciated, for she was used to working for a self-contained employer. Thomas Tranter explained exactly what was wanted, told her to get in touch with him if ever she was in any difficulty and then left her to get on with the job.

Some days she never saw him at all. On others, he would suddenly come across her kneeling on the library floor or standing on some steps, clipboard in hand. Sometimes he would pop his head round the door of the nearby small office, where she sat at the desk Monica

Arrowby had used, surrounded by notes and files which she did her best to keep in order. She had always been tidy-minded. It was second nature to her and she imagined it was one of the reasons why she had suited Gerald Frobisher, who was apt to leave his books and belongings here, there and everywhere, relying on her to tell him where everything was.

It surprised Jessica that Monica had not been more meticulous, especially as she felt that Tom Tranter was not a man to suffer fools gladly; but she could only suppose that her predecessor's main forte had been her knowledge of the history of the house and that her activities as librarian had been something which she had agreed to undertake during the winter months, almost as a sideline. Her desk certainly did not reveal itself as that of a woman with any secretarial qualifications. There appeared to be no arrangement. In its drawers dried-up biros and broken elastic bands surfaced amongst a variety of papers, while discarded shorthand notebooks — in which Monica had scribbled in barely decipherable longhand — lay underneath pristine writing paper and envelopes. It occurred to Jessica that possibly someone more suitable should have been employed to catalogue the library and one day, when she had more time, she resolved to make order out of Monica's chaos. However, having glanced cursorily at what appeared to be detritus, she crammed it all for the moment into two large boxes, so that she would have more space to organise and concentrate on matters in hand.

Each evening, as she said goodnight to the security guard and set off to drive back to King's Folly, Jessica felt pleasantly satisfied with her day's work. She knew she was beginning to get on top of it, even if slowly and, as she reached the end of her ten-mile journey, she looked forward to being greeted by Chancy and Gracie and the welcoming drink which she knew would be waiting for her.

Although improvements to the property were still in progress, Jessica had been made very comfortable in a wing of the farmhouse itself, with her own bedroom, bathroom and sitting-room. It had been decided that no official bookings would be accepted until August — when several art courses were planned — but by word of mouth and imaginative advertising, the place had already started to attract interest. Demands for brochures kept arriving and stray sightseers often appeared, directed by local inhabitants who seemed to have adopted a 'wait and see' attitude to all that was going on.

While Jessica continued to regret the departure of Mercedes and her son and granddaughter, she sometimes came across one or two people she knew. Dr Pinnegar seemed pleased to see her when she called at his surgery one Saturday for a prescription for more blood pressure pills, warning her, jocularly, not to let herself get buried beneath too many books; and one day she met Sidney Yates outside the Whistling Pig. He shook her hand warmly, telling her that his wife was 'coming along now', although she had had to give up any idea of returning to the Tourist Office. "Still," he said, "she's got the house to herself at last." "Your father-in-law?" Jessica queried, tentatively. "Oh, Bill . . ." Sidney's face hardened. "Believe it or not, his wife took him back. She's got some job over Minehead way, cooking for a new holiday camp. They live in a caravan and fight like cats and dogs, it's said. But, whatever happens, I've told Edna he's not to set foot in our house again. 'Twere a bad business all round last year and no mistake."

A bad business. Jessica surmised that this was still the general attitude in the district. Country folk did not forget. There might be a new broom sweeping through King's Folly, but could it ever sweep away all the dust created by the mysterious death of Leo King?

A month or so after her arrival, Jessica and Chancy decided to ask Caroline if she would care to come down for a weekend and they were delighted when she accepted the invitation. On arrival, Jessica was amazed at the further improvement in her looks. After a rapturous reunion with Gracie, she entered into the life of King's Folly with enthusiasm, complimenting Chancy on all his plans, glad to find the garden still seemed to be a going concern and thrilled to see the new road edging its way across the old bumpy track.

"Chancy's getting on well, isn't he?" she remarked to Jessica, when they were alone one evening in her sitting-room. "He's doing all the things I always hoped to do, but never got around to . . ." There was not a hint of envy or regret in her voice.

"Would you ever consider . . . ?" Jessica began, but was quickly forestalled.

"Coming back, you mean? Oh, no. That part of my life's over. Jessica, don't get me wrong and it's early days, but . . ."

"You've met someone else?" It was Jessica's turn to make the interruption.

Caroline stared at her. "Yes, a friend of Richard. His name's Michael Woodley. He's nice. He understands how I feel. I'm still hoping we'll find out exactly how Leo died. But . . . how did you guess?"

"Just by looking at you," Jessica replied.

As the summer wore on and she realised, sadly, that her job was slowly coming to an end, Jessica decided to do something about the two boxes of assorted oddments which she had put aside at the beginning of her assignment. There was a strong temptation to discard everything without a second look, for she doubted that there could be anything of importance left but, ever conscientious, she requested some dustbin liners and set to work. It was an irksome task but she was determined to see it through.

At one point in her labours, Colonel Tranter looked in and became, unusually for him, quite expansive as he expressed his gratitude for all she had done; but, after he had gone, Jessica felt that she knew no more about him than when she had arrived. Their relationship had been curiously impersonal, reminiscent of that which she had had with Gerald Frobisher.

It was not until her final day, when she was scrabbling to pick up items which had missed their destination in the waiting sacks, that she chanced upon one of Monica's old notebooks lying on the floor. It had fallen open at a page on which was scrawled, 'Dear Tom'. Jessica, never having got anywhere near to being on Christian name terms with him, was intrigued, although she realised that he and Monica would have known each other a great deal longer.

Remaining on her knees and with increasing curiosity amongst all the crossings-out and insertions she was able to decipher:

In case anything happens to me, I am writing this letter for you to deal with as you think fit.

At the inquest into the death of the late Leonard King, I stated that I had passed another car near the scene of the tragedy on that fateful night. There was no such car. It was a fabrication.

You will recall that I had left you an hour earlier, after you had told me that, because of your wife's deteriorating health, our relationship must cease. You said you intended to retire and that, as far as possible, we must not see each other again. During the last few years you had become my whole life. I did not know how I was going to be able to drive home without some sort of help. I stopped at the nearest pub and had a double brandy, perhaps two, I can't remember exactly. Drinking had already become an increasing problem, one which I have tried to hide from you and everyone else.

Had anyone been wrongly accused of Leonard King's death, I like to think I would have confessed immediately. As it remained unsolved, I remained silent. I never noticed him standing on the bridge until it was too late. I only knew I had struck the body of a tall man with my nearside bumper. I stopped and ran back, but he had disappeared in the water. After a few minutes I drove on. I knew my mother would be waiting for me. As you know, any late return had to be accounted for.

When the police enquiries started and I realised whom it was I had hit, I came forward and later committed perjury at the inquest. I realised they were looking for cars which might have been in the district at the time and mine, having been driven all around the countryside by my late father for so many years, would have been spotted by someone or other.

I have acted this way for the sake of the only person I have ever loved, for

that of his wife and my own mother.
May God forgive my transgression.

M

Holding the notebook in trembling
hands, Jessica felt faint and slightly sick.
She was in possession of the answer she
had been seeking for so long, yet now
that she had it she did not know what
to do. Presumably, Monica had written
a fair copy and had given or sent it to
Tom Tranter. Maybe she had forgotten
or had died before tearing up her original
draft. There was no date on it. Had she
had a presentiment of death? Had he,
on receipt, decided to keep quiet for
the sake of his wife, his own reputation
and that of Monica's? Confused, Jessica
made an attempt to get up, staggered
and passed out.

When she came round, she found
herself lying on a small couch in a
corner of the room and Tom Tranter
sitting beside her. Monica's notebook
still open in his hand. "The doctor
and Mr Lennox will be here soon, Mrs
Milroy," he said. "I fear you have had a
. . . shock."

She tried to speak but the words refused to come.

"Miss Arrowby's mother," he continued, and even in her confused state, she was surprised how formally he referred to his late mistress, "has now lost her memory. She is senile. My wife has not long to live. As soon as Valerie passes on, I shall do what I always intended to do. I shall inform the police."

She wanted to say thank you but, still unable to articulate, she could only feel grateful that his last words were overheard by Chancy and Dr Pinnegar, who had just come into the room.

Addendum

In the latter half of 1993, several announcements appeared in *The Daily Telegraph*, all disparate yet each pertaining to a certain course of events which had taken place during the previous twelve months:

DEATHS

TRANTER. — *On July 24, Valerie, beloved wife of Thomas Gordon, after a long illness bravely borne. Funeral at All Saints, Long Buckley, 2.30 p.m. Thursday July 29th. Donations, if desired, to cancer research . . .*

MILROY. *On August 7, peacefully, following a stroke, Jessica Frances. Loving and much loved grandmother of Jason. Sadly missed by Marianne, Caroline and Chancy. Funeral private. No flowers or letters please.*

MARRIAGES

Woodley – Frayne. On September 1st, at Kensington and Chelsea Register Office,

Michael James, elder son of Eleanor and the late Sir Anthony Woodley, to Caroline Susan.

No further reporting ever appeared in the press concerning the death of Leonard King but, at the end of October, on one of the Feature pages, there appeared a large photograph of Gracie and Chancy outside King's Folly, underneath which was a splendid write-up, starting: *A new venture in the West Country has begun with remarkable success . . .*